# Impossible,
## Looking Fo...
### To Run E...

'*That's* the ad you should run!' Kayla said. 'And if you want to hire someone else to help you around here, I'll gladly place it.'

'Wrong,' Jack retorted. 'The ad should read "Good-looking, smart guy with sense of humour looking for temporary help. Emotional types need not apply."'

'Emotional types?' Kayla repeated in disbelief. 'I'm not emotional. You're impossible! I'm irritated by your preposterous demands—'

'Irritated? Oh, I think you're past that! Try furious and bossy.'

Too furious to say another word, she turned to leave.

Afterwards, Kayla couldn't be sure if Jack reached out to prevent her from leaving...or to open the door and boot her out. Either way, he tottered on his crutches, tumbled into her arms—and she landed in trouble!

Dear Reader,

This month, there are more strong and sexy men in Silhouette Desire®!

In *Nobody's Princess* by talented, award-winning author Jennifer Greene, meet April's MAN OF THE MONTH, Alex Brennan. Regan Stuart was determined to stay single—until gorgeous Alex changed her mind... And in Cathie Linz's *Husband Needed*, Jack Elliott reluctantly offers to trade his single days for married nights...

Nobody creates a mouthwatering hero quite like Sara Orwig, and in her latest book, *Babes in Arms*, she brings us Colin Whitefeather, a tough rancher who shows his tender side when he helps bring a tiny newborn into the world. And talking of babies, *Do You Take This Child?* is the last book in Marie Ferrarella's THE BABY OF THE MONTH CLUB. When the long-absent dad-to-be bursts into the delivery room, Sheila Pollack says 'I do'—*between* huffs and puffs!

Peggy Moreland's delightful mini-series, WIVES WANTED! continues with *A Little Texas Two-Step* and finally, *Wind River Ranch* is a real treat from Jackie Merritt.

In Silhouette Desire, you'll always find the most irresistible men around! So, enjoy!

The Editors

# Husband Needed

## CATHIE LINZ

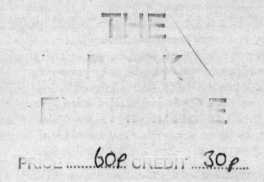

*Silhouette, Silhouette Desire and Colophon
are registered trademarks of Harlequin Books S.A.,
used under licence.*

*First published in Great Britain 1998
Silhouette Books, Eton House, 18-24 Paradise Road,
Richmond, Surrey TW9 1SR*

ISBN 0 373 76098 1

22-9804

*Printed and bound in Great Britain
by Mackays of Chatham PLC, Chatham*

# CATHIE LINZ

left her career in a university law library to become a best-selling author of over thirty contemporary romances.

This award-winning author often uses comic mishaps from her own trips as inspiration for her stories, but she set this book in her own back yard—her home town of Chicago. After travelling, Cathie is always glad to return to her family, her two cats, her computer and her cookie jar.

**Other novels by Cathie Linz**

*Silhouette Desire®*

Change of Heart
A Friend in Need
As Good as Gold
Adam's Way
Smiles
Handyman
Smooth Sailing
Flirting with Trouble
Male Ordered Bride
Escapades
Midnight Ice
Bridal Blues
A Wife in Time
*Michael's Baby
*Seducing Hunter
*Abbie and the Cowboy

*Three Weddings and a Gift*

# One

Someone was trying to break into his place!

Jack Elliott heard the doorknob to his apartment rattle again, ever so slightly. He'd already gotten robbed once since moving up to the north side of Chicago, he wasn't about to have it happen twice.

Sure, the building had a doorman as a security measure, but that hadn't prevented the last robbery—probably because Ernie the Doorman had the IQ of a snail.

The doorknob rattled once more and then turned slowly. There wasn't time to call the police. There wasn't time to think, just to act.

Unfortunately, his broken leg prevented Jack from acting very quickly. Despite a life often spent living at the edge, this was the first time Jack had ever broken a bone and he was *not* a happy camper. He'd been swearing at his crutches all morning, but now they looked like they might come in handy.

Standing up and hanging on to the bookcase beside the door with one hand, Jack raised one of the wooden crutches over his head, ready to bash whoever walked through his front door. A man had a right to protect his own property.

The door opened slowly, furtively...

Giving a war cry that would have done a warlord proud, Jack brought the crutch down...only to belatedly realize the burglar was a woman with a kid! Their ensuing screams were even noisier than *his* had been.

Swearing loudly and succinctly, Jack somehow managed to avoid hitting either one of them. Instead he swung his crutch to the far right, poking a hole clear through the wallboard next to the door. He'd suspected the walls in this place were paper thin, now he knew it to be a fact.

"Are you crazy?" the female intruder screeched at him even as she scooped up her little girl and protectively held her close. "You could have killed us!"

"You bring a kid along with you to break into my apartment and you have the nerve to call *me* crazy?" Jack yelled back at her, hanging on to the bookcase for balance. He *hated* being at a physical disadvantage this way, and his mobility was even further hampered by the fact that one of his crutches was now imbedded in his apartment wall.

"See what you've done? You've upset my daughter," the woman said with an accusing glare.

"Upset? *Upset?*" Jack repeated in disbelief. "You better answer my questions and answer them fast or I'll show you upset! Who are you and why the hell were you breaking in here?"

"I didn't break in, I have a key," the woman retorted, having soothed her daughter into silence while continuing to shield the little one with her own body.

Now that the kid had stopped her ear-splitting screams, Jack could finally think. The woman didn't look like a thief, with her big blue eyes and curtain of honey brown hair that fell around her shoulders like waves of silk. But then looks could be deceiving.

"Where did you get a key?" he demanded.

"From your uncle, Ralph Enteman."

Jack frowned. Now that he thought about it, his uncle had called him yesterday afternoon and said something about sending over a surprise.

"I'm assuming you *are* Jack Elliott?" the woman continued.

"That's right. And you are?"

"Kayla White."

"Am I supposed to know you?"

"Your uncle hired me."

"Great," Jack groaned, remembering the last person his uncle had hired for him, an "exotic dancer" he'd sent over on Jack's last birthday. "Tell him thanks, but I'm not interested," he said wearily. "You can just head right back where you came from."

"Excuse me?"

"There's the door. I want you on the other side of it."

"I don't think you understand…" she began, when he interrupted her.

"Look, honey, it's nothing personal, although I can't believe a girl like you would bring your kid with you when you're on a job like this. But hey, that's your business."

"You have a problem with me bringing my daughter with me?" Kayla repeated. "And what do you mean by 'a girl like me'? I'm a woman, Mr. Elliott, not a girl."

"I noticed. Look, I'm just not in the mood, okay?"

Kayla frowned at him. "In the mood for what?"

"For—" remembering there was a kid present, Jack substituted, "—fun and games."

Her look became tinged with suspicion. "Just what is it that you think I'm here for?"

"Why don't *you* tell *me?*" he countered.

"As I said, your uncle hired my company…"

Jack interrupted her again. "You *own* a company that does this kind of thing?"

Actually she co-owned it with her best friend, Diane, but Kayla saw no purpose in going into details like that at this point. So instead she merely said, "That's right."

"So you must have a lot of…experience?"

"You could say that."

"Do you go out a lot on jobs like this?"

"Every day."

After giving her a head-to-toe once-over, Jack wondered if maybe he was being a little hasty here. She might not be as busty as he liked his women, but she wasn't half-bad. The plaid skirt she wore stopped above her knees, and the black tights clinging to her legs accentuated their shapely length. She was almost dressed like a preppie college coed, probably a popular costume in her line of work. College coeds and nurses were big—that last exotic dancer had been dressed as a nurse. The only thing out of place was the little girl Kayla was holding.

"Anyway," Kayla continued, "your uncle told me that you needed some help temporarily, what with your broken leg. He assured me he'd already spoken to you about all this."

"He lied," Jack said.

"He didn't tell you I was coming over?"

"My uncle told me that he had a surprise for me, but that's all he said." Jack belatedly registered that she'd mentioned something about his needing help, which got him to wondering exactly what kind of help she was talking about. The possibilities were erotic and endless. But the woman had a kid with her. This was one of the strangest setups he'd seen. "I can't believe he gave you a key to get in."

"He wasn't sure if you'd be home."

"Where else am I gonna be with a busted leg?"

"The doorman downstairs told me that you'd gone out."

"Yeah, well, Ernie is several cards short of a full deck," Jack retorted. "So tell me, what exactly is it that you do? I mean, you really don't find it inhibiting to have your daughter with you on jobs like this?"

"No. Why should I?"

"Hey, far be it from me to cast the first stone, but I would have thought…I mean…it kind of breaks the mood, you know what I mean?"

"No, I don't have a clue what you mean," she replied. "Do you have something against kids?"

"There's a time and a place for everything and I don't think this is the time or the place for a kid to be watching her mother…do…whatever it is you do. Just how exotic do you get?"

"Exotic?"

"Isn't that the politically correct term for what you do? Exotic dancing, instead of stripping?"

Kayla's eyes widened and her mouth dropped open before she icily stated, "I am *not* an exotic dancer!"

"What would *you* call what you do?"

"Running errands. I own a company called Errands Unlimited. We do a variety of things, Mr. Elliott, but dancing and/or stripping is not one of them!"

"Hey, it was a natural mistake for me to make." Jack held out a hand, before remembering that he needed that hand to hang on to the bookcase. He only narrowly saved himself from falling flat on his face.

But Kayla seemed unmoved by his difficulty. She was too busy spitting fire at him, her voice sizzling with anger. "A natural mistake? Really? I'd love to hear how you figure that."

"The last surprise my uncle sent over was an exotic dancer for my birthday. So naturally I thought…"

"You thought wrong."

The haughty look Kayla gave Jack made him feel like something that had crawled out from under a rock. It was January and the weather outside was beyond chilly, it was downright frigid—but even so, the expression in Kayla's blue eyes lowered the already cool temperature in his apartment by about twenty degrees. She had classy features, icy eyes and a passionate voice, not to mention pretty damn good legs. She was fire, coated with ice, and she didn't seem the least bit impressed with him; that alone made her stand out among the women he knew.

Okay, so he wasn't exactly looking his best, but at least his gray running shorts accommodated the cast on his right leg. His sweatshirt had Northwestern University Wildcats emblazoned across the chest, bracketed by the spaghetti sauce he'd spilled on it when he'd tried carrying a plate of spaghetti from the kitchen to the living room earlier. Should he tell her that he looked better cleaned up?

As he watched her, Kayla efficiently disengaged the wooden crutch from the wall and handed it to him. "Here. I think you might need this."

The crutch seemed to mock him, underscoring his temporary lack of independence. Irritably taking it from her, he demanded, "So why did you bring your kid with you?"

The kid—who, after her first ear-piercing screams, had been remarkably quiet up to this point—promptly burst into tears again and hid her face in the crook of her mother's neck, making Jack feel like an even worse heel.

"All I did was ask a simple question—" he began.

"You's mean!" the little girl shouted from the safety of her mother's arms.

"Shhh, sweetie, it'll be okay," Kayla murmured in a soothing voice. "This is Mr. Elliott, and he's not as bad as he seems."

"Gee, thanks," Jack muttered.

"If you'll just give me the list, Mr. Elliott, I'll get to work," Kayla briskly stated.

Jack stared at her blankly. "The list?"

"The list of errands you want me to run."

He took exception to her maternal tone of voice. "Listen, I already have a mother, I don't need—"

"It's my understanding that you've already driven your mother to distraction," she interrupted him to say. "That's why your uncle hired me."

Jack glared at her. "Okay, so I don't like people fussing over me."

"I'll remember that. Your uncle felt that you would prefer someone objective assisting you rather than being 'fussed over' as you put it."

Actually what Jack's uncle had said was "My nephew is *impossible!* If you can handle him, you can manage anything and I can assure you that I'll throw more work your way than you'll know what to do with." As a member of the Chicago Board of Trade, Mr. Enteman could throw a *lot* of work her way with other traders who were too busy to handle the details of their daily lives. This could be the break she and Diane were waiting for, their first big account.

Meanwhile, Jack was reconsidering his position. He supposed there were worse things than being waited on hand

and foot by a beautiful woman like Kayla. He'd noticed that she wasn't wearing a wedding ring. Which meant what? That she was divorced? Available?

"We got off on the wrong foot here, no pun intended," he said, fitting the padded handle of the crutch under his arm. "What do you say we start over again? How about telling me your daughter's name?"

"It's Ashley."

"Hey, Ashley, I'm sorry I was yelling before," Jack said in his most charming voice, the one he'd been told on more than one occasion could charm the wings off an angel.

But his charm apparently didn't work on *little girls,* since Ashley refused to even look at him, just burrowing her face even further into her mother's shoulder.

Not that Jack should complain, since the kid's actions did manage to shift the neckline of the black angora sweater Kayla was wearing so that it displayed the intriguing hollows of her collarbone and the soft curve of a shoulder. A flickering flame of awareness teased his senses and warmed his appetite.

His gaze leisurely traveled upward, from the creamy skin of her throat over a chin that looked like it could be stubborn, to her lips.... *Very* nice lips. Her cheeks were flushed, with anger or attraction? When his eyes finally reached hers, he got his answer—she met his perusal head-on. She was looking at him as if he were a low-life and she a queen. Jack wasn't sure whether to be insulted or intrigued.

Women had always found him attractive—he wasn't conceited about it, he was simply accustomed to it. He had gray eyes and a way with women; both were mere facts. Over the years there were plenty of women who'd found him to be irresistible.

But not this one. This one was eyeing him with complete indifference and just a twinge of impatience. Jack saw no hint of attraction in Kayla's blue eyes, not a smidgen of sympathy at his being laid up with a broken leg. Maybe it was time to bring up the fact that he was a firefighter—that usually got women's attention.

"Did my uncle tell you that I was injured in the line of duty?" Jack asked her.

"No."

Didn't the woman have any curiosity? he irritably wondered. "I'm a firefighter."

"That's nice."

Nice? *Nice?!* That's it? Okay, so swinging his crutch at her had not made the best of first impressions. But he could make up for that. "Look, why don't you and your daughter sit down while I write up the list. As you can see, it takes me a while to get around." He'd never had to use the sympathy angle before, but hey—if it worked…

It didn't.

"You moved fast enough swinging that crutch of yours," Kayla replied.

Ah, so she wasn't going to make this easy on him, was she? Okay. That was fine by Jack. He hadn't had a challenge like this in years. Well, actually, he'd *never* had a challenge quite like this, but he was man enough to rise to the occasion.

And the way her angora sweater clung to her curves did indeed make a certain part of his anatomy rise. She was tall, only about four or five inches shorter than his own six feet. And she wasn't wearing heels. In fact, she was wearing practical-looking black flats.

"In those clothes, you don't look old enough to have a daughter," he murmured.

Kayla narrowed her eyes at him. She knew damn well

he was practicing his charm on her. She also knew that he was aggravated it wasn't working. Good. It served him right—for scaring the heck out of her, swinging his crutch at her and nearly decapitating her.

It didn't matter that he had the most intriguing eyes she'd ever seen—a blend of blue and gray. They were like smoke. In contrast, his dark lashes and eyebrows were a commanding combination. His hair was equally dark and somewhat on the wild side, which she had a feeling matched his own personality. Somewhat on the wild side.

He had the powerful build of a man who was used to physical activity. His shoulders were exceptionally broad, straining against the sweatshirt he wore. And the running shorts displayed his muscular legs, the calf muscles well developed. *All* of him was well developed, for that matter.

But if he thought she was going to melt, now that he'd turned on the sex appeal—the heated looks from those smoky eyes, the devilish grin from lips a sculptor would have loved—he was sadly mistaken. She'd already been put through the grinder by a pro. Her ex-husband, Bruce, had been as good-looking as they came. She'd fallen in love with him at first sight and had scarcely been able to believe her luck when he'd finally asked her out. It had been her first month at college. By the end of the year, she'd dropped out and they'd gotten married. The next five years had flown by as she'd been busy working to put her husband through medical school—only to have him dump her when he'd finished his internship.

That had been nearly three years ago and the hurt was still there, if not the love. Kayla had used part of the divorce settlement she'd received to start up Errands Unlimited with Diane. After all, Kayla had been running Bruce's errands throughout their marriage. Yet as a working mother, she knew how little time there was in a day, and had often wished she'd been able to afford to hire someone to do the million and one things that needed to be done in a day that had too few hours.

And now she had the chance to prove herself to Jack's uncle, with the reward being her first big account. Yes, this job was an important one, not that Kayla intended to let Jack know that.

She intended to keep things strictly professional. She didn't care how attractive the man was. Her ex-husband had been hunk material. On the outside. She'd discovered too late that he was just a jerk at heart.

"The list," she reminded Jack.

"Right."

As Kayla watched him struggle to maneuver himself over to the couch she had to steel herself against giving in to her immediate impulse to rush over and help him. It wasn't in her nature to just stand by when someone needed assistance.

"Mommy, you's huggin' me too hard," Ashley complained.

"Sorry, baby." Kayla kissed her daughter's forehead. "We'll be going soon…"

A string of curses filled the air as Jack hit his big toe on the leg of the coffee table.

"Mr. Elliott, I'd appreciate it if you'd watch your language around my daughter!"

The outraged primness of Kayla's voice made Jack want to…kiss her. She had the kind of mouth for it. Soft and full. Downright lush.

Shifting Ashley from one hip to the other, Kayla said, "If you can't write up the list now, I'll come back later…."

Not wanting her to leave yet, Jack said, "No, let's do this now." He sank onto the couch. Wondering why it was so lumpy, he tugged a pile of newspapers, several T-shirts, and an empty pizza carton out from under his thigh.

His apartment would never win any housekeeping awards on the best of days, which this was not. Shoving the pizza carton onto an already overladen coffee table, Jack said, "First off, I need food. There's nothing in the kitchen except for a bag of lentils. I don't know how the hell they got into my house. I hate lentils."

"Then write up a grocery list and I'll pick up some food for you. You'll also have to give me the money."

"That's the second thing on my list. I don't have any cash." Jack ran an impatient hand through his hair, further ruffling the dark strands and intensifying his wild buccaneer look. "I have to go to the bank or an ATM. I mean, *you'll* have to go to the bank or an ATM."

"Why don't you just make me out a check instead?"

"That's number three on the list. I'm out of checks. I meant to order more from the bank, but I never got around to it...."

Kayla's sigh threatened to set him off again. So did the way she was looking around his living room, as if expecting rats to come crawling out of the woodwork. He might be messy, but he was no slob. But before he could say so, she spoke first.

"I'll advance you the money, but please be advised that this is a one-time occurrence. Your uncle is paying for my services, but not for the materials supplied—not for the groceries bought or the dry cleaning picked up...."

"Lady, I haven't had anything dry cleaned since 1990," Jack retorted, his anger rising at the sound of her long-suffering tone of voice. It made him feel like an idiot. *She* made him feel like an idiot. The problem was, she also intrigued him, tempted him and aroused him. A lot! More each time he looked at her.

"If you're going to make a list, you'll need something to write with," she briskly said, coming closer to hand him a pen with her free hand.

As their fingers met, a spark sizzled. Given his earlier attraction to her, Jack was expecting it—but apparently Kayla wasn't, because she shot him a startled look. He saw a glimpse of an answering awareness in her eyes. It was just a glimpse, but it was enough. For now. She wasn't unmoved.

Jack smiled. Suddenly his immediate future was looking a lot brighter. Here he'd been feeling sorry for himself, moping around the place because of his busted leg and the projected four-week recovery period until he could return to work. But now it looked like there was a good chance that things could get *real* interesting in that time period. Really interesting, thanks to a woman with big blue eyes and a frosty manner.

Even given her unexpected presence, he still hated being laid up this way. It put a real crimp in his style, not to mention the fact that he had too much to do to be slowed down.

Jack didn't realize he'd spoken that last thought aloud until Kayla said, "That's what I'm here for. To help you."

So why was it that Jack had the sudden feeling that Kayla would end up doing more harm than good to his bachelor life?

# Two

"So, what did you think of my nephew?" Ralph Enteman asked Kayla as she drove away from Jack's building. Ralph had called her on her cellular phone.

"He's everything you said he was…and more," she replied.

Recognizing the irritation in her voice, Ralph said, "You're not going to quit, are you?"

"Of course not! In fact, I'm on my way now to get your nephew some groceries and other necessities." In her opinion, Jack could definitely also use some common courtesy and patience with a little cooperation thrown in. Unfortunately none of those things could be picked up at any store. Talk about being obstinate…the man could give lessons to a mule!

As if reading her mind, Ralph said, "I did try to warn ᵃᵗ Jack could be stubborn."

s, you did. But apparently you didn't warn *him* that

I was coming to his apartment. Jack mistook me for some-one else. He tried to smack me over the head with his crutch.''

"Oh no! I know he's got a temper, but I never thought he'd do anything violent."

Kayla felt compelled to clarify. "In his defense, he thought I was trying to break into his apartment."

"Oh. Well then, his reaction makes sense. Someone *did* break in and rob him a few months back, although that neighborhood is much better than where he used to live. The thing is, Jack isn't a man to just sit around and do nothing if threatened."

"Believe me, I wasn't at all threatening. Quite the op-posite." Kayla was tempted to add that she'd had her daughter with her, but she wasn't sure what Ralph's re-action would be. After all, Jack hadn't been that pleased to see Ashley.

But Kayla had a schedule and nothing messed with it, even handsome firefighters like Jack. Today was Wednes-day, and on Wednesdays Kayla kept Ashley with her until one p.m., when she dropped her off at the Windy City Day Care Center. One of the things Kayla liked about her work was the ability to take Ashley with her now and then. Most workdays Kayla did leave her daughter in child care, but there were certain days, like today, when they shared time together.

Stopping at a red light, Kayla shot a smile over to Ash-ley, who was strapped into the car seat and happily talking to her favorite toy—a rather battered teddy bear named Hugs. The bear was even older than three-year-old Ashley, because Kayla had bought it for her the day she'd found out she was pregnant. There had been some tough times in the intervening years, and the toy's brown fur had now faded to a dark beige from numerous washings.

"Anyway, I'm sorry Jack upset you," Ralph was saying.

"He didn't upset me," Kayla assured him. After all, it wouldn't do for her client to think that she was easily distracted. She wanted him to appreciate her calmness and reliability. She wanted him to think of her as a woman who got the job done. "We got everything settled, no problem."

"Good. I'm glad to hear that."

After hanging up her cellular phone, Kayla told herself that she hadn't lied to Ralph. As far as she was concerned, everything *was* settled between Jack and her. And that sizzle of attraction she'd felt when she'd handed him her pen had been a figment of her imagination. She refused to even consider any other explanation.

"Anyone home?" This time Kayla made sure to announce her return to Jack's apartment. She'd tried ringing the buzzer, but there had been no reply. And after his former blunder, Kayla didn't trust Ernie the Doorman anymore. The fact that Ernie had asked her if she was Jack's "latest" hadn't exactly endeared him to her, either.

"This is your second time here today, not that I pry into other people's business," Ernie had told her in a monotone so deadpan it would put a caffeine-freak to sleep. What little hair Ernie had was carefully combed back from his forehead in a futile attempt to give him the image of having more hair than he actually did. His uniform fit his hefty build so snugly that the buttons were straining, as if ready to launch themselves across the lobby.

Despite his disclaimer about prying into other people's business, Kayla had sensed that Ernie had been more than willing to give her the lowdown on Jack, but she hadn't stayed to chat. It was already after three, and she had other clients and other errands to run before calling it a day. But she had accepted Ernie's help in transporting several bags of groceries up to Jack's front door.

"Jack, it's Kayla," she called out as she pushed the door open a little further. She had two plastic bags of food in one hand. The list of groceries he'd given her had cost her nearly eighty dollars, and most of it was junk food. "I've got your groceries. Anyone here? I'm not a burglar or belly dancer…" she couldn't resist adding with a grin. "Hello?"

She made it into the living room without Jack taking any kamikaze swings at her with his crutch. In fact, she didn't see any sign of him. For a moment she panicked, wondering if he'd fallen and hurt himself. An image flashed into her mind of him lying in the bedroom, injured, unable to get up. Then she registered the sound of the shower running.

Her mental image switched from him lying on the bedroom floor, to him lying in the bathroom, his chest bare…perhaps even *all* of him bare.

"Oh, great, that's very helpful," she muttered under her breath. "Having steamy fantasies about your client when the poor man is injured and could be in trouble."

So what should she do? Knock on the bathroom door and make sure he was okay? Let him know she was there? She certainly didn't want him walking out of the bathroom nude or anything. He seemed the type to do just that. Yet she didn't want to startle him, either. He might slip in the shower and break his other leg.

Putting her ear to the door, she heard him singing. Okay, that meant he wasn't in trouble. In fact, his voice wasn't half-bad. *Neither was the rest of him.* The rebellious thought slipped into her mind before she could stop it.

"That's enough of that," she muttered under her breath. "Get your mind out of the shower!"

In the end, Kayla decided to write a note telling him she

was there. She taped it to the bathroom door. She'd no sooner done that than the phone started ringing. Expecting an answering machine to pick up, she waited for seven rings before the noise drove her crazy, forcing her to answer it herself. She'd never been able to just ignore a ringing phone—after all, it might be an important call.

"Mr. Elliott's residence," she said briskly, juggling the six-pack of soda she was trying to place into the fridge at the same time.

"Who is this?" a woman's voice demanded. "Where is Jack?"

Wishing now that she hadn't answered the phone, Kayla said, "He's in the shower."

"In the shower?" the woman repeated in disbelief. "What kind of answer is that?"

"The best one I've got," Kayla retorted. "May I tell him who's calling?"

"Misty. And have him call me back as soon as he gets out!"

"Fine. Does he have your number?"

"Honey, he knows me inside and out," the woman purred before hanging up.

Kayla had no sooner hung up the phone than it rang again. She'd automatically picked it up before realizing what she'd done. "Hello?" she said before belatedly tacking on, "Elliott residence."

"Oh, my, you're not Jack!" Caller number two had a husky female voice that was made all the more sultry by a Southern accent.

"That's right," Kayla said cheerfully. "I'm not Jack."

"Which girl are you?" the woman asked. "You don't sound like the snippy attorney who was chasing him last week. And you're not the waitress with the English accent, either."

Kayla began wondering if that was how Jack had broken his leg, from being chased by endless lines of women.

"Mr. Elliott is unavailable at the moment," Kayla stated. "May I take a message for him?"

"Tell him Mandy is worried about him and willing to drop everything to come on over there to take care of him. He just has to say the word and I'll be right there."

"I'll tell him."

By the time Jack came out of the bathroom, wearing nothing but a smile and a pair of running shorts, Kayla had collected a stack of nearly half a dozen messages—all from women with names that rhymed.

"You got calls from Misty and Mandy, Tammy and Sammy, Barbie and Bobbie," she said, trying to keep a straight face.

"What are you laughing at?" he demanded defensively.

"Nothing." Her earlier amusement disappeared as the details of his appearance belatedly sank in with her.

He'd looked good before but now…now he was raw masculinity incarnate. More of him was bare than was covered. He was a throwback to another age, a time when men survived by their physical strengths.

Although solidly built, there wasn't an ounce of extra flesh on him. Dark hair covered his chest, trailing down from collarbone to navel, but not so thick that she couldn't see the ridges of muscles beneath. He radiated presence and power—a knight minus his shining armor.

Which left her as what…a damsel in distress? Realizing she'd been holding her breath since he'd walked in the kitchen, she belatedly inhaled. She could smell the fresh scent of his soap. Her gaze fastened on the single droplet of water slowly meandering down toward the waistband of his running shorts, which clung to his still-damp lower torso.

The silence was deafening as Kayla heard the increased pounding of her own heartbeat. She saw the way his chest rose and fell. Was he breathing faster, too? Her eyes lifted to meet his. Only then did she realize how pale he was.

Quickly gathering her wits, Kayla asked, "Uh…are you supposed to be taking a shower so soon after breaking your leg? When *did* you break your leg, anyway?"

"Yesterday."

"Yesterday!" His answer evaporated her steamy fantasies as concern took their place. "And you're singing in the shower today? Are you crazy?"

"Probably," he muttered, grimacing at the pain shooting up his right leg.

"A three-year-old would have more sense! Here, you'd better sit down before you fall down," she said, scooting a kitchen chair over to him.

"I'm not an invalid," he snapped.

"No. You're an idiot!" The words were out of her mouth before she could stop them.

She immediately clapped her hand to her lips with such a look of guilt that Jack had to smile.

"No, don't hold back," he teased her. "Go ahead and tell me what you *really* think."

"I think you should sit down."

"I'll never get used to these stupid crutches by sitting down."

"What's your hurry? Didn't the doctor tell you to take things easy for the first few days?"

"I've had emergency medical training. I know what I'm doing. What are your qualifications?" he growled irritably. Willing himself past the pain wasn't working, and the pain medication the doctor had prescribed made him too damn groggy.

"I broke my leg once. When I was ten," Kayla told him.

"Oh, and I suppose that makes you an expert?"

"Are you always this grouchy or does a broken leg bring out the worst in you?" she inquired in exasperation. Remembering that he hated anyone fussing over him, she deliberately focused her attention on unpacking the remaining groceries.

"Very funny."

"Not really," Kayla replied, opening a cabinet and finding it empty except for... She held up two plastic bags of dried beans. "Having nothing to eat in the kitchen but lentils, now that's funny."

"I don't know how they even got in the kitchen," Jack muttered. Deciding enough time had passed to make his point—that he wasn't a weakling who obeyed orders—he carefully made his way the three steps to the kitchen chair, hoping it didn't look like he collapsed into it. "I hate lentils," he said, before reaching over and snagging a clean T-shirt from the laundry basket on the kitchen table.

"Maybe one of your girlfriends brought them for you," Kayla said, trying not to notice the way his muscles rippled as he lifted his arms to tug the T-shirt over his head. The movement ruffled his still-damp dark hair, adding to his roguish appearance.

"None of my girlfriends know how to cook," Jack replied.

"Really? You mean you weren't attracted to them because of their culinary talents?"

He didn't look amused.

Delighted to be provoking him for a change, Kayla continued. "You know, I've heard there's safety in numbers, but I've never seen such a remarkable example of it before."

"What is that supposed to mean?"

"Come on. Misty, Mandy, Tammy, Bambi..."

"I don't know a Bambi," Jack inserted, enjoying the way her blue eyes lit up with humor. He'd only seen that intense shade of blue once before, in a kitten he'd befriended as a kid. Eyes so full of life.

"No Bambi, huh?" Kayla said. "Well, I'm sure it won't take you long to remedy that. How can you keep them all apart with names so similar?"

"That's not a problem. Randi has long red hair and the biggest pair of...eyes you ever saw."

"Never mind." The humor in Kayla's eyes was replaced with a flash of something else, something he couldn't identify. "Forget I asked."

"No way. The least I can do is satisfy your...curiosity."

"That's all you're gonna satisfy, buster," she muttered under her breath.

"What did you say?"

"I was just talking to myself."

"Lonely people do that a lot, I hear."

"I'm *not* lonely," she denied.

"No?"

"No. I have a daughter and I lead a very full life."

"Even if you're not an exotic dancer?"

His mocking voice sneaked under her defenses, making its way to her heart like a shot of whiskey. Not that she had much experience with whiskey. She was more the milk shake type herself.

"I still can't believe you ever thought that," she said.

"Why not?"

"Because. I mean, I'm not...I don't have the right kind of body.... Never mind."

Jack grinned. "For what it's worth, I think you *definitely* have the right kind of body. The kind I like."

"From the number of women who called you, it sounds as if you like *all* kinds of female bodies," she tartly retorted.

"Hey, there's always room for one more."

"I don't care for crowds." Her voice got that prim tone again, the one that made him want to kiss her.

"I'm not wild about crowds, either," he murmured.

"You couldn't prove it by those calls."

"Ah, but one-on-one is always best, don't you think so?"

"I think this discussion has gotten way out of hand," she declared in a no-nonsense tone of voice.

"And here I was, thinking things were just getting interesting.... Wait a second. What's that?" Jack demanded as she pulled a six-pack out of the grocery bag.

"Beer."

"It's not the right kind of beer. That's not what I wrote on the list."

"They didn't carry that imported brand. The liquor clerk told me this one would taste the same."

"Well, he lied. It doesn't. One is ale, this is just a pale imitation."

"Fine—" she snatched the six-pack back from him "—I'll pick up your imported beer tomorrow."

"And these aren't the right kind of beer nuts, either," Jack grumbled, eyeing the can he'd removed from one of the plastic bags still littering the floor. "These are honey roasted. I wanted salted."

"I had no idea I was dealing with such a gourmet."

He raised an eyebrow at her. "I know what I like. Do you have a problem with that?"

"I'm not the one with a problem," she muttered under her breath.

"Implying that I am?" he retorted,

"You're the one with the broken leg."

"What a brilliant observation."

She'd *observed* plenty of other things about him, like the way his dark hair tumbled over his forehead as it dried, the intensity of his smoky eyes, the breadth of his shoulders—swimmer's shoulders. And then there was his mouth. When he'd grinned at her a few minutes ago, it had been like watching the sun come out. Crinkly laugh lines had suddenly appeared at the corners of his lips and his eyes. The gleam of devilish humor in his gray eyes made them seem even more awesome than usual.

Belatedly realizing he'd caught her staring at him, she hurriedly said, "So exactly how did you break your leg?"

"I told you, I broke it in the line of duty. You didn't seem too interested in hearing the details this morning."

"That's because you rattled me."

"Really?"

"Who wouldn't be rattled when a madman comes at them, waving a crutch and shouting like a banshee?"

"Why do I get the feeling that there isn't much that rattles you?"

"I'll take that as a compliment. And you still haven't answered my question about how you broke your leg."

"Would you believe I broke it falling out of bed at the firehouse?"

"That depends."

"On what?"

"On whether or not that's the truth."

"It's one version of it."

"Truth doesn't have versions."

"Sure it does. Ask any cop. You get three witnesses and you'll get three different versions of the truth."

"So what's your version?"

"I got clumsy." Fighting fire left no place for being

clumsy. "Fire is a jealous taskmaster," he murmured, almost as if he were talking to himself. "She doesn't like it when you take your attention off her, even for a second."

"So fire is a female?"

Jack nodded.

In exasperation, she said, "Why is it that anything disastrous is female—hurricanes and now fires?"

"Hurricanes are named after guys now," he pointed out. "But something as beautiful and powerful as fire has to be female. She's like a living thing that eats...and hates. And in her eyes you're nothing more than fuel. That's all you are. Fuel."

Kayla shivered. There was just something so matter-of-fact in his voice. "How can you talk about it that way? So calmly?"

"Because I fight fire. It's what I do."

"And doing it broke your leg?"

He shrugged. "I told you, I got clumsy. You've seen me on these crutches and you've got to agree, I'm not the most graceful guy you've ever seen."

Not the most graceful, no—but certainly the most powerful. Yet for all of his strength, she experienced this sudden need to look after him. "Did you get your cast wet when you took your shower?"

"Nope. I put a garbage bag around it because the doc said to keep it dry."

"What other orders did the doctor give you yesterday?"

"Hey, no one gives me orders outside of the firehouse."

Kayla sighed. Her instincts were right. This guy definitely needed a keeper. "Meaning you probably ignored whatever orders the doctor gave you, right? That was real bright. Do you enjoy being in pain?"

"Want me to tell you what I enjoy?" Jack countered, his gaze focused on her lush lips.

"I already know."

"You do?"

She nodded and held up a bag of corn chips. "Junk food."

"Among other things. Lots of other things."

Kayla refused to be distracted. "Did the doctor give you a prescription?"

Jack nodded.

"Let me guess. You didn't get it filled, did you."

The look on his face said it all.

"What is it about men that makes them so stupid?" she demanded in annoyed exasperation. "Are they born that way or is it learned behavior? I think they're born that way," Kayla answered herself. "It's some sort of defective gene, the same one that makes men refuse to ask directions or read instructions."

"What do we need to read instructions for?"

"To get the job done faster."

"There are plenty of times when slower is better," he murmured, the look he gave her making it clear what those times were.

"Oh, I see. So slower is better when you're in pain from a broken leg? Sure, that makes sense. Why take medication to make you feel better, right? I mean, that would be admitting that you're human. That once in a blue moon you might need some help. Heaven forbid that should ever happen!"

Jack glared at her. His humor wasn't helped by the fact that his leg was really throbbing in earnest now.

Seeing the pain etched on his face, Kayla felt remorse for yelling at Jack, even though he did deserve it. "If you'll give me the doctor's prescription, I'll go get it filled for you," she said quietly.

"Forget it. The stuff made me too groggy."

"How do you know? You haven't even taken it yet."

"They gave me one at the hospital. I've got some over-the-counter stuff around here someplace. I'll take a couple of those."

"You bet you will," she said, spying the bottle of analgesics near the kitchen sink. "What would you like to drink with it? Water or soda?"

"I'd say beer, if you'd gotten the right brand."

"You're not supposed to drink beer when taking these," she told him. "Where do you keep your glasses?" she asked as she searched through the cabinets.

"I don't have any right now. Just give me the can of soda."

She did.

Jack took the pills, tilting back his head as he drank half the can in one go. He knew she was watching him. She'd been watching him since he'd gotten out of the shower. But there was a wariness in her gaze that didn't sit well with him. Never one to beat around the bush, Jack said, "So who was the guy who gave you such a warped view of men?"

"I don't have a warped view of men," she immediately denied. "If anything, I have a clearer view than most."

"And why is that?"

"Because I was married."

"I guessed that much. And now you're...?"

"Divorced." She reached for another bag of groceries, noting that the chocolate mint ice cream had almost melted. Normally she had a system to putting away groceries, one that involved putting away the perishables first. But Jack's appearance, half-naked and still dripping from his shower, had flustered her.

"What happened?"

"What do you mean what happened?" she repeated,

worrying that he'd noticed the melting ice cream and somehow guessed he was the reason for it.

"With your marriage."

"I'd rather not talk about it."

"You're not over him yet?"

"What makes you say that?"

"The look in your eyes. Kitten blue eyes. Ah, now they're going all frosty. And when you laugh, they kind of shimmer."

"I'll bet you say that to all your girlfriends," she declared before realizing what company that put her in. "Not that I'm one of your girlfriends," she hurriedly clarified.

"Not yet," Jack murmured.

"Not ever." Pulling her scattered thoughts together, Kayla reached into her purse. "The bank put a rush on getting your new checks in. Until then, here are some temporary checks. The cash you wanted with your ATM card is in this envelope. And here's the receipt for the groceries—the total was seventy-three sixteen. You can make me out a check for that." She handed him the temporary checks, receipt and a pen.

"How do I make it out?" he asked.

"To Errands Unlimited. And don't forget to call your friends back. You know, Misty and the gang...."

"They can wait. First I'm calling Vito's Pizza for dinner."

"Are you going to be okay here tonight?"

"Why?" Jack countered. "Are you offering to stay with me?"

"No. Misty and the gang were more than willing to come over and hold your hand."

He shot her a devilish smile, one that was slow and sultry. "They just have a thing for a man in a uniform."

"You're not in a uniform now," she noted with a telling look at his bare legs.

"So you noticed."

"It's hard not to," she muttered. "Aren't you cold?"

"No. Are you?"

Since she was fanning herself with the grocery receipt, she could hardly say yes. Instead she said, "I'm not the one wearing shorts."

"More's the pity," Jack replied, his gaze traveling down her legs.

It was all Kayla could do not to tug on the hem of her skirt. The look he'd just given her made her feel as if she were wearing black fishnet stockings instead of perfectly respectable tights. "I'm leaving," she firmly declared. "You're clearly too stubborn to have anything happen to you, so I'm sure you'll be fine on your own." Not that she thought he'd be on his own very long.

"Hey, come back tomorrow and we'll do this again," Jack called out after her.

The sound of the door slamming was his only reply.


"So, buddy, tell me again why I had to spend my morning off patching this hole in your wall? Or maybe we should start with how you put a hole in the wall in the first place," Boomer Laudermilk told Jack the next morning. Boomer was a ten-year veteran of the Chicago Fire Department, the same as Jack, and was one of Jack's closest friends.

"It was a simple misunderstanding," Jack replied.

"Yeah, right. Like the time the captain caught you short-sheeting his bed."

"Something like that."

"Which still doesn't tell me much."

"I smashed the tip of my crutch through the wallboard."

Boomer's bushy, blond eyebrow lifted almost to his hairline. "In a bad mood, were you?"

"I thought she was breaking in—"

Boomer interrupted him. "*She?* You didn't tell me there was a woman involved. Man, I shoulda guessed. There's always a woman involved where you're concerned. So what happened this time? You fall for a female cat burglar?"

"I haven't fallen for anyone! Certainly not a bossy errand girl named Kayla, even if she does have the best legs I've ever seen and incredibly big baby blue eyes that show her every emotion."

"Uh-oh, buddy, this doesn't sound good."

"She's got a kid," Jack declared, as if that said it all.

"Is that a problem?"

Jack shrugged.

"Don't your parents run a day care center?" Boomer asked.

Jack nodded.

"Then I'd think you'd be used to kids."

"You'd think wrong. My folks are good with kids. Not me."

"So what are you going to do about this Kayla woman you're not falling for?" Boomer asked.

"Damned if I know."

Kayla was running late when she got to Jack's apartment Thursday afternoon. It didn't help that she'd had to stop three places before finding Jack's stupid imported ale and the right brand of salted beer nuts. On her way out yesterday, she'd given Ernie the Doorman the rejects. Ernie had responded by smiling at her, or at least she'd assumed the

slight movement at the corner of his mouth was a smile—
he wasn't exactly the demonstrative type.

Now Jack was another matter entirely. He certainly let
you know how he was feeling. She'd called a cleaning
service to stop by this morning, only to have them call her
back and say that Jack had thrown a fit and refused to let
them in. It had taken Kayla fifteen minutes to calm down
the cleaning service owner, a necessity since Kayla often
worked with them. No, she was *not* feeling kindly toward
Jack at the moment.

And those feelings took another nosedive when she saw
the note taped to his front door. It had her name on it, as
well as the name of the pizza place around the corner.
Apparently Jack didn't believe in using blank paper for
writing when he could make do with odds and ends.

Along with her name, he'd written half a dozen errands
for her to run—including buying a five-dollar lotto ticket,
picking up the latest video releases, buying a package of
men's white jockey shorts in size thirty-four as well as a
bottle of pricy perfume.

It sounded as if the man had something special planned.

So why did that bother her? Why should she care what
he did with Misty or Mandy or any other woman? She
didn't care. It just irked her that he'd written the note as
if she were a peon and he the great lord ordering her about.
Not to mention her aggravation at the way he'd treated the
cleaning service people this morning, after she'd gone to
all that trouble to get him squeezed in. If Jack thought she
was cleaning up after him, he was sadly mistaken.

She rang the bell and pounded on the door. When that
got no response, she was about to get out her key when
Jack finally answered the door. Seeing how pale he was,
she asked, ''What happened to you?''

''What do you mean what happened to me?'' he

growled. "I broke my damned stupid leg, that's what hap- pened. And then I was kept up most of the night with women calling me, trying out their phone-nurse routines, asking me what I'd do if I couldn't work as a firefighter anymore. What the hell kind of question is that to ask a man?"

Since he was weaving on the crutches like a drunken sailor on shore leave, Kayla said, "Maybe you should sit down—"

"I'm fine," he growled.

"You don't have to snap my head off," she said, in- explicably hurt by his curtness. "I was just trying to help you…"

"I don't need any help." His words were gritty with anger and frustration. This was only his third day in the cast and already he was going nuts.

"Right. I can tell you're doing just peachy on your own," Kayla mockingly noted, waving her hand at the living room strewn with clothes, newspapers, dirty dishes and empty bottles and cans. "Why did you send away the cleaning people?"

"Because I don't want strangers around. Besides, I told you I hate people fussing over me," he growled.

"Yes, well, I hate people fainting on me," she retorted, "and that's what you're going to do if you don't take it easy."

"I've never passed out in my life."

"There's always a first time, big boy."

"Listen, *little girl,*" Jack shot back, "don't order me around!"

"Hey, don't yell at me because your girlfriends kept you up all night" was her immediate comeback.

An x-rated reply was on the tip of his tongue, but he bit it back because the truth was that Kayla had been the one who had kept him *up* all night—in *every* sense of the word. Jack hadn't been able to get her off his mind and that was driving him out of his mind.

"That wasn't yelling. THIS IS YELLING," he shouted, working up a good head of steam. "If this is the way you treat your other clients, I'm surprised you're not out of business. You couldn't even buy a simple bottle of beer and some beer nuts without screwing up!"

Kayla didn't care if this job might lead to good things for her company, *nobody* was going to talk to her that way! "If you don't stop yelling at me, I'm going to break your other leg!"

"This isn't going to work," Jack declared. "I'm going to hire someone else."

"*You* didn't hire me, your Uncle Ralph did."

Jack waved her words away as if they were of no importance. "I'll get someone else."

"Good luck. You're so impossible no one would work for you! Your uncle warned me about you."

"Yeah, well, he didn't warn *me* about *you*. He should have known better. He knows I don't like bossy women."

"You want to hire someone else? Fine. I'll even help you find them," Kayla stated, her anger fiery hot at his accusation that she was bossy. Retrieving her ever-handy notebook from her oversize purse, she said, "I'll write up the help-wanted ad for you. Let's see…how about 'impossible, irritable, arrogant man looking for blindly devoted slave to run errands for him at any time of the day or night. Salary—not enough. Benefits—none. No appreciation, no courtesy.'"

"Wrong. The ad should read 'Good-looking, smart, good-natured guy with great sense of humor looking for temporary help. Emotional types need not apply.'"

"Emotional types?" she repeated in disbelief. "I'm *not*

emotional! You're just impossible! You'd try the patience of a saint.''

''You're claiming to be a saint?''

''Of course not. If I were, I wouldn't be irritated by your preposterous demands and outlandish expectations....''

''Irritated? Oh, I think you went past *irritated* some time ago,'' Jack retorted. ''Try furious and bossy.''

''Stop calling mc bossy!''

''Or what?'' he taunted her.

Too furious to say another word, she turned to leave.

Afterward Kayla couldn't be sure if Jack reached out a hand to prevent her from leaving...or to open the door to boot her out.

Either way, he tottered on his crutches and ended up flattening her against the closed door—tumbling her into his arms.

# Three

Kayla instinctively put her arms around Jack's waist to steady him. His breath was warm and minty against her cheek as he braced his arms against the door, his hands on either side of her head. His lower torso was intimately pressed against hers so that she could feel every bone and sinew of his muscular frame.

She saw the hunger flare in his incredible smoky eyes even as she felt the throbbing of his arousal through his running shorts. Her coat was open, and her denim skirt wasn't thick enough to provide any protection against the heated intensity of his powerful body.

Not that she wanted protection. She wanted him to kiss her. He did, slowly but fiercely consuming her as if he had all the time in the world to enjoy every millimeter of her mouth and couldn't wait a second longer to do so.

This was no first kiss. There was no tentativeness, no awkwardness. Instead there was an uncontrollable passion, flaring with wild abandon. What her lips asked for, his tongue took. His mouth was slanted ravenously across hers as each velvety stroke of his tongue fueled the fire deep within her.

Kayla hung on for dear life. But she was no passive partner. She melted against him, wrapping her arms more tightly around his waist, wrapping her tongue around his in an erotic tousle that was as elemental as fire itself.

The blood was pounding through her body. In his arms she was a different person, forgetting everything but him. She shivered with excitement as she felt his fingertips gliding up her thigh, lifting the hem of her skirt. Fiery licks of pleasure danced over her skin wherever he touched her.

Things got so intense that her knees shook, her head swam and there was a buzzing in her ears. A loud buzzing....

It wasn't until Jack lifted his lips from hers that reality returned. She snatched her hands away from him as if burned.

"What was that?" Kayla whispered, holding her trembling fingers to her lips.

"The door buzzer."

"No. I meant...*that*...between us—" she waved her hand toward him. "Where did that come from?"

"Okay, I admit, you turned me on..."

She blushed. "I wasn't talking about anatomy. I meant, we hardly know each other. You're a client." She raised her hands to her burning cheeks as she muttered, "I don't do things like this."

The intercom buzzer sounded again, more stridently this time.

"You better get that," she said, leaning down to get Jack's fallen crutches for him. As she did so, her forehead almost brushed against his thighs.

Muttering under his breath, he took the crutches and made his way the few feet to the intercom. "What?" Jack growled into the speaker.

"This is Ernie, your doorman. I just thought you might be interested in knowing that a traffic officer is stopped farther down the street and is issuing parking tickets."

"Why the hell would I care?"

"Because your visitor double-parked her minivan in front of the building."

"Did you double-park out front?" Jack asked Kayla.

"Yes! I was only going to stay a minute, drop off your beer and beer nuts. I've got to go!"

"Wait! You'll come back, right?" Seeing her hesitation, Jack said, "You're not really going to quit, are you? You didn't seem like the type to give up easily."

"I don't aim on giving up...anything," Kayla quietly informed him before closing the door in his face.

By the time Kayla went to pick up her daughter at the day care center that evening, she felt as if she'd been run over by a truck. She hadn't been fast enough to avoid getting a parking ticket at Jack's, and her day had continued to go downhill from there. The Shellburgers' dry cleaning had gotten lost and it had taken her an hour at the cleaners to retrieve it. A simple exchange at the shoe store for Sally Galanter had also turned into a fiasco.

And then there was The Kiss—the one Kayla was determined to wipe from her mind. No amount of determination could completely erase the steamy memories, however.

Still, it helped when Kayla walked into the day care center and switched into "Mommy" mode.

But she'd no sooner stepped into the building when her beeper went off. Checking it, she recognized Diane's number. Unfortunately Kayla's cellular phone battery had just gone out on her not an hour before, forcing her to ask the day care owner, Corky O'Malley, if she could use her phone.

"Sure," Corky cheerfully replied. Her short dark hair was generously peppered with white, creating a salt-and-pepper look that reminded Kayla of her own mother. There the similarity ended, however. Corky was much more loving and giving than Kayla's mother had ever been. "Come on back and use the phone in my office. It's quieter there."

"Thanks." Kayla quickly called Diane and reported in, assuring her that she had indeed found the missing dry cleaning.

"Rough day?" Corky asked sympathetically once Kayla had hung up.

"You could say that. There's one client in particular who is the most demanding man I've ever met. You wouldn't believe..."

Kayla's voice faded away as she stared in amazement at the framed photo on Corky's desk. She'd never used Corky's phone before, but she had certainly seen the man in that photo before. He'd been kissing her senseless not three hours ago.

"What wouldn't I believe?" Corky prompted her.

"Who is that in the picture, if you don't mind my asking?"

"I don't mind at all," Corky replied. "That's my son, Jack."

"Jack Elliott?"

"Why, yes. Do you know him?"

"But your name is O'Malley," Kayla stuttered before gathering her wits. "I'm sorry, that was rude of me. It's really none of my business."

"We adopted Jack when he was thirteen. He claimed

that Jack O'Malley sounded like the name of a bar, so he kept Elliott. Actually, I think the truth was that Jack felt it would be disloyal to his natural parents to discard their name since they'd only died a few years before. Not that he'd ever say that. Ah, but he's a stubborn one, is our Jack.''

"You can say that again," Kayla muttered.

"So you do know him. Oh, my!" Corky grinned. "Could Jack be that impossible client you were referring to?"

Kayla thought about denying it before guiltily nodding. "I'm afraid so."

"Don't feel bad about it, dear. I've said worse about him myself. I tried to help him right after he broke his leg, but he was like a bear. I'm his mother and *I* couldn't cope with him when I went over there. He said I fussed too much. Are you the surprise my brother Ralph said he was getting for Jack?"

"Yes, I am. I gather Ralph has gotten surprises for Jack before," she said before blushing, wondering if his mom knew about the exotic dancer Ralph had sent over.

Apparently Corky did, because she grinned before saying, "Ralph thinks very highly of Jack. So do I. Don't get me wrong, I love him dearly. He's courageous, loyal, caring. He likes helping others and is always the first to face any challenge. In fact, the word *impossible* is not in Jack's vocabulary. But he does have a few faults."

"He seems very popular with women."

Corky nodded. "He always has been, ever since he was in junior high school. They flock around him like bees to honey. He's played the field for so long that I wonder if he'll ever settle down. Not that he wouldn't make a good husband. He would. I just want him to be happy."

"This is just so weird, your being his mom and running Ashley's day care center."

"It's a small world, hmm?"

"So have you learned any way of dealing with Jack's stubbornness?"

"I'm afraid not. The good news is that he comes to his senses sooner or later. There's just no hurrying him along. How bad was he?"

"On a scale of one to ten, he was about an eight."

"And his apartment?" Corky asked. "Did it still look like a bomb had gone off in it?" Seeing her hesitation, Corky added, "You don't have to lie, believe me, nothing can be as bad as his room used to be when he was a teenager. Funny how he always knew where everything was, though. He's really not a total slob, and I raised him to be quite a good cook. You should try his Irish stew sometime."

"I don't know about that…" Kayla muttered.

"So what did he do to upset you today?"

Kayla couldn't exactly tell her that Jack had kissed her as if she were the only woman in the world for him and that she'd kissed him back with the same heated intensity. So she focused on his other misdemeanors instead. "I hired a cleaning service to stop by his place but he refused to let them in. And I got a parking ticket for double-parking in front of his building to drop off this stupid imported beer he likes."

"Ah, blame the beer on my husband, Sean. He got Jack going on that Irish brand of ale."

"Mommy, Mommy!" Ashley yelled from outside the office. "I's here. Look!" She waved a large piece of paper, half-crumpled in her excitement. "I got stars!"

"So you did, sweetie." Kayla leaned down to give her

daughter a big hug before smoothing out Ashley's artwork. "Let me see."

"It's a monster. Like that mean man who walks with trees. I bet he kilt those trees. Put a spell on them. Made them fly through the wall."

"Those aren't trees, they're called crutches and the man was using them because he broke his leg."

"How come he broke his leg?"

"It was an accident."

"Like the time I spilt my milk all over?"

"Something like that."

"I don' like him," Ashley declared. "Hugs don' like him, neither." She lifted her ever-present teddy bear as if to prove her point.

"Is my son Jack the monster Ashley has been talking about for the past two days?" Corky asked.

"There was a slight misunderstanding when we first arrived," Kayla replied. "He thought I was trying to break in.... Anyway, it all worked out in the end."

"Jack never has been very good with little ones," Corky admitted regretfully. "He never stops by the day care center when the kids are here. I'm not sure why he avoids children, perhaps they remind him of a time when he was young and vulnerable."

"I's hungry now, Mommy," Ashley announced. "Hugs is hungry, too. Hugs wants choclotts for dinner."

"Hugs has to eat what we eat and we don't eat chocolate for dinner," Kayla stated. "We're having spaghetti."

"I want mine naked," Ashley said.

"She doesn't like spaghetti sauce," Kayla explained for Corky's benefit.

"An' I don' like the monster man, neither!" Ashley declared.

* * *

Later that night, after she'd put Ashley and Hugs to bed, Kayla was getting ready for bed herself when she discovered a crinkled piece of paper in the pocket of her denim skirt. It was the list of errands Jack had given her.

She touched the bold strokes of his writing with her fingertip even as she remembered his last words before she'd left. *You'll come back, right? You're not really going to quit, are you? You didn't seem like the type to give up easily.*

It wasn't professional to leave him hanging, uncertain whether or not she was going to fulfill her obligations.

*Fulfill...* Ah yes, and how that word got her to thinking about other things. Like the way he kissed. The feel of him in her arms, his body intimately pressed against hers.

It had been like dancing in the heart of a flame. She'd never felt that way before, despite the fact that she'd been married all those years.

That didn't mean she had any intention of getting romantically involved with Jack, however. What had happened between them was destined to be a one-time fluke. She was strong enough to resist temptation, even temptation as forceful as Jack. There was more at stake here— this was an important account, and while she wasn't willing to put up with verbal abuse from Jack, she wasn't going to be a wimp and quit because she couldn't control her own hormones.

She'd stay on the job. She'd prove to herself and to Jack that she could handle this situation.

She had her hand on the phone, ready to dial Jack's number, when the phone rang.

"Kayla, it's Bruce."

The sound of her ex-husband's voice was enough to make Kayla's stomach sink to her toes. He never called unless he wanted something.

"I just wanted to remind you that I won't be able to visit Ashley this weekend because I've got a medical convention in Orlando," Bruce continued.

"This is the first I've heard of it."

"Come on, I told you about it last month."

He hadn't, but Kayla wasn't about to get into an argument with him. That would be playing right into Bruce's hands. He relished arguing with her, it seemed to provide him some kind of sick pleasure.

"This is the second time this month that you're waiving your visitation rights," she reminded him.

"That's because you won't be flexible and let me see Ashley during the week." His imperious voice grated on her nerves.

"The divorce decree gave you weekend visitation rights."

"I could go back to court if you get difficult," Bruce said.

It was a threat he'd used before, but even so, now that he'd married Tanya Weldon and had her wealthy Oak Brook family on his side, Kayla couldn't dismiss his threats.

"I've told you before how much Tanya's family loves Ashley," Bruce went on to add. "And since we found out that Tanya can't have kids of her own…"

*She can't have my daughter!* The words screamed through Kayla's head. Ashley isn't something Bruce's rich wife can buy, like that Mercedes she just had to have last month.

"Think about it," Bruce said before hanging up, leaving Kayla a nervous wreck.

Despite her best efforts, her emotional state was apparent in her voice when the phone rang again seconds later.

"H-h-hello?" She hated the nervous stutter.

"Kayla? You sound funny. What's wrong?" Jack demanded. "Are you okay? What's wrong?" he repeated.

"How did you get my home phone number?"

"You're listed in the phone book. Now tell me, what's wrong?"

"You don't want to know."

"Am I going to have to come over there and drag it out of you?" His muttered comment contained more frustration than menace. "What's the problem?"

"Gee, where do I start?" she mockingly pondered while fingering the telephone cord with her free hand. "Maybe I should begin with the impossible client who threw a cleaning crew out this morning, a cleaning crew I do a lot of work with, I might add."

"Yeah, well I've given things some thought and—"

"You've decided to let the cleaning crew come back?"

"No, this has nothing to do with the cleaning crew. This has to do with the fact that I'm not really your client. My uncle hired you, as you've often pointed out. So kissing me wasn't breaking some cardinal rule or anything."

"*You* kissed *me*," she reminded him.

"And you shouldn't treat it as if we did something illegal."

"Speaking of which, I got a ticket for double-parking in front of your building."

"I'm sorry about that."

"Me, too." She couldn't really afford that chunk of change out of this week's budget.

"But not about kissing you. I'm not sorry about that."

"I'm so glad one of us isn't," she retorted.

"Now you're sounding more like your old self."

"You've only known me two days. That's not long enough to know what my old self is like."

"Sure it is. I'm a good judge of people."

"Sure you are." She had to smile as she continued fingering the phone cord. "That's why you thought I was an exotic dancer when I first came to your place."

"Actually first I thought you were a burglar, remember?"

"My daughter remembers, all right. And she wasn't amused."

"Yeah, I got that impression."

"I suppose I should tell you before Corky does, that Ashley goes to your mom's day care center."

"You're kidding?" There was a moment of silence before Jack asked, "So I suppose the two of you talked about me?"

"You think Corky and I had nothing better to do?"

"I think you talked about me. What I want to know is, what did she say?"

"That you're incredibly stubborn."

"Yeah and what else?"

"Why? What are you afraid she said?"

"Afraid? Me? The word is not in my vocabulary."

"That's not what I heard."

"What did you hear?" His voice suddenly had a hard edge to it.

"I heard that children scare you," she teased him.

"Little rug rats don't scare me," he scoffed, but there was no amusement in his inflection. "But apparently I scare them. I didn't mean to make your daughter cry."

"I know you didn't."

"So are you giving up on me?" he bluntly asked her.

"Can you give me one good reason why I shouldn't?"

"That kiss."

"I should think that would be a reason to avoid you."

"Ah, but then you'd admit to being afraid of me. And you're not." The caressive warmth of his voice flowed over her. "You might be afraid of whatever it is that's between us, but you're not afraid of me."

"Oh? And how do you know that?"

"Because you threatened to break my other leg, remember?"

"I shouldn't have said that," she said regretfully. "I should have reacted in a more mature manner."

"I like the way you reacted. I also like the way you kiss. The question is, what do you like?"

"Peace and quiet. And I don't think that's something you can offer me."

"Probably not," he acknowledged. "But I can give you something even better."

"And what's that?"

"My Irish stew and a broad shoulder to lean on."

The idea of really being able to lean on someone else for strength actually brought tears to her eyes. There were certainly times when Kayla wished there was someone else to help her make the million and one decisions involved with raising a child. But Jack was even more of a novice in that department than she was. She couldn't afford any more mistakes in her life.

"Come on, what do you say?" Jack softly prompted her.

"I say that it's best if we keep things businesslike between us. Are you going to be home tomorrow?"

"Sure. Where else would I go? We've got ice-coated snow out there and they're expecting more later this week."

"The weather forecasters are full of prunes," Kayla retorted. "They said we'd get a huge snowstorm today and we barely got a dusting tonight. This is the fifth time a storm has missed us this winter. I'm beginning to think they're just using the threat of snowstorms to raise their ratings."

"What made you so cynical? Or should I say who?"

"You should *say* good night. It's late."

"I'll see you tomorrow."

Yes, he would. And she could only hope that by then she had her act together. Because that kiss had already proved how vulnerable she was to Jack's particular brand of charm. And with Bruce breathing down her neck, this was no time for her to mess up.

"He did what?" Diane asked Kayla in the tiny offices of Errands Unlimited the next morning. The office space was only large enough for two desks, a computer, two filing cabinets, three chairs and half a dozen Boston ferns—a passion of Diane's. The single window had a western exposure and provided plenty of sunshine, which was a blessing in the winter and a pain in the summer.

"He kicked out the cleaning crew," Kayla repeated.

"No, I meant the part before that. I could have sworn you said Jack Elliott kissed you."

"He did."

"The swine." This was Diane's favorite expression of disgust, culled from her many viewings of the Beatles' classic movie *A Hard Day's Night*. Her mom had been an avid Beatles fan and had raised her daughter to be the same.

Diane had grown up next door to Kayla and they'd known each other since they were both six. It had been Diane's idea for Kayla to join her in this business venture. Diane liked to say that she provided the verve and Kayla provided the common sense. They'd each put up equal amounts of start-up money, and this year their hard work was finally starting to pay off.

"How dare he take advantage of you that way!"

"Diane, the guy has a broken leg. It wasn't exactly a situation of being taken advantage of."

"Uh-oh. That means you liked it. Jeez, Kayla do you know what this means?"

"That I'm in trouble?"

"This is the first guy you've liked kissing since your divorce."

"Keeping track, are you?"

"You bet I am. I want you to be as happy as George and I are."

"Impossible. You two were made for each other."

"And what about this Jack? What's he like?"

"The complete opposite of me. He's popular with women, has them coming out of the woodwork practically. Not that you can see much of the woodwork, his place is pretty messy at the moment. His mom runs the day care center I take Ashley to, do you believe that?"

"So Jack must be good with kids, right?"

"Not really," Kayla ruefully admitted. "He didn't exactly make a good first impression with Ashley."

"I remember, you told me he tried to clobber you with his crutch."

"That's right."

"He didn't try that again to get you to kiss him, did he?" Diane demanded.

"Of course not."

"Do you want me to take over his account?"

"No, I can handle this," Kayla said firmly. "I have a plan."

"Oh yeah? This I've got to hear."

"I'm going to be pleasant and cheerful. No more arguments and no more kisses. I'm going to keep my distance."

"Sounds like a plan," Diane agreed. "We'll see how well it works."

Kayla's plan did work. For the next eight days—she was counting—she didn't have a single argument with Jack. No kisses, either. She remained pleasant and cheerful despite the fact that Jack was neither, although he didn't blow up at her again as he had before.

Instead he'd give her these long heated looks that were potent enough to melt steel. Kayla told herself she should have been insulted, but she wasn't. Instead she was enticed, tempted to daydream about things she couldn't have but kept on wanting, anyway. A knight in shining armor, one who would slay a few dragons for her, just to give her a break from slaying them all by herself.

She should know better. Knights, like the dinosaurs Ashley liked so much, were extinct.

"You're staring at me again," she said in exasperation on the ninth day as she handed Jack the receipts for his paid utility bills. They were sitting in his living room, he on the couch while she perched on a chair a respectable distance away. Not an especially romantic setting. But the heated hunger in his eyes was enough to transform their prosaic setting into a romantic, candlelit idyll. The space between them practically sizzled with something she was afraid to name, a powerful blend of anticipation and sensual tension.

"I like looking at you," Jack declared, his voice as powerfully seductive as his gaze had been. "Is there a law against that?"

"There should be," she muttered under her breath.

"What did you say?"

"That you should be more careful about the due dates on your utility bills. They were just about ready to turn off your electricity."

"I've had other things on my mind." His look told her that he'd had *her* on his mind.

"Ernie told me that you went out yesterday."

"I was getting cabin fever being cooped up in here for days," Jack said.

"It's been twelve days."

"Feels like ninety," he muttered.

"So did you enjoy getting out?"

"Oh, yeah, it was a real blast," he noted sarcastically. "I had to rest on Ernie's chair in the lobby. Then I nearly broke my other leg when I went outside and slid on an icy patch on the sidewalk."

"Did you hurt anything?"

"Just my pride."

"And heaven knows you've got plenty of that."

"I'm not the only one," Jack retorted. "You've got plenty of pride yourself."

"It comes in handy sometimes," Kayla replied. Changing the subject, she added, "The place looks much better since you decided to let the cleaning service in."

"That was a one-shot deal," he warned her. "I just got a little behind on stuff. I'm not a total slob."

"So your mom told me."

"Aha! I *knew* you two talked about me."

"I still can't get over the fact that she's your mom," Kayla admitted without thinking.

"Why? Because we're so different? That happens when you're adopted."

"I understand your parents died in a car accident."

"Yeah, when I was nine."

"I'm sorry."

He shrugged off her sympathy with a wolfish smile. "I'll tell you what *I'm* sorry about."

"What?"

"The fact that you're way over there and I'm over here." Jack's smile turned downright wicked as he patted the couch seat next to him invitingly. He looked so darn cocky and sure of himself. And sexy as all get-out.

"What's the matter?" Kayla mockingly retorted. "Have the other women in your life taken off on you?"

"I don't care about any other women," Jack replied.

But Kayla just laughed and shook her head at him. "You're good, I'll give you that."

Jack loved her laugh. She was wearing her preppie outfit again, the one with the angora sweater and black tights. He didn't know which skirt he liked better, this plaid one or the denim one she'd worn when he'd kissed her.

He only knew he couldn't go much longer without kissing her again.

Jack was used to moving fast—it was a requirement when fighting fire. So was a clear head.

But he hadn't been really lucid since meeting Kayla, and he certainly hadn't had a sane thought since kissing her. He'd had plenty of cold showers, though. In fact, he'd gone through an entire box of garbage bags to protect his cast.

Too bad there was no way to protect his peace of mind. Only one thing would do that—having Kayla in his bed. And that prospect raised almost as many problems as it solved. Because Kayla wasn't the type of woman you went to bed with and then let go. She was the kind you got serious about and getting serious had never been his forte.

"I'll match your bet and raise you ten bucks," Jack said, before reaching into a nearby bowl for a handful of beer nuts. The poker game was a weekly ritual with some of the guys from the firehouse, who treated it with all the reverence of a religious ceremony.

This week the game was supposed to take place at Boomer's place, but it was being painted today, so they'd come to Jack's apartment instead.

"How can you drink that stuff?" Sam Cernigliano asked Jack, grimacing and pointing to the Irish ale. "It tastes like camel urine."

"Drunk much of that, have you?" Jack countered.

"You should talk, Sam," Boomer inserted. "Those cheap cigars you smoke are enough to make a camel sick."

"Like those skinny imitations you smoke are any better," Sam retorted.

"At least they don't turn the air blue."

"Nah, your language does that. Read 'em and weep, fellas," Sam said as he set down his cards.

Sure enough, the sound of Boomer's creative curses filled the air.

"Now you know why he's called Boomer," Jack noted at the roaring sound of his friend's voice. "And, Sam, usually that would be a very good hand. But last I heard, a royal flush beats a full house."

Now Sam's curses joined Boomer's.

Jack just leaned forward to rake in his haul and smiled.

"You've got the devil's own luck," Sam complained. "You've got more women than you know what to do with and now you clean us out at cards. I tell ya, it's not fair."

Jack's smile widened as he said, "Life's not fair, Sam."

"You know how many times I've broken a bone?" Sam asked. "Go ahead, ask me."

"I don't have to ask you," Jack retorted, "you've told us this story about a million times."

"Six times. Six times I've broken bones. And never once did a busty redhead sign my cast. How many women have signed that thing now?"

"Over a dozen, at last count," Boomer, a bachelor without Jack's golden touch, said gloomily.

Jack joined in his friend's laughter even as he remembered how Kayla had refused to add her signature to the many already there. *I don't like crowds,* she'd reminded him.

"Yeah, well, we've all got our burdens to bear," Jack said, both in answer to Boomer's comment and to his own turbulent thoughts. "Speaking of which, you're awful quiet tonight, Darnell."

"I'm worried about my wife," the young black man admitted.

"The baby's not due for another three weeks. You've got plenty of time yet," Sam, the oldest of the foursome, said with the authority of one who knows. "I've got five kids, I know about these things."

"It looks like the snow is starting to really come down out there." Darnell's voice remained worried.

"You've got a four-wheel-drive vehicle that could make it through two feet of snow," Jack pointed out.

"And you've got your beeper turned on so your wife can reach you," Boomer noted. "And her mother is staying with her while you're here. What more could you want?"

As if on cue, Darnell's beeper went off. He lurched from the metal folding chair and raced to the phone like a sprint runner.

"Yes?" he panted into the phone once he reached his wife. "Judas H. Priest, yes, yes, I'll be right there!" Turning to his buddies, Darnell shouted, "She's in labor! I gotta go. I'm gonna be a daddy!" Darnell dropped the phone into the salsa dip as he headed for the door, without his coat.

"Yo, Darnell! Hang on a second. Here." Sam grabbed his arm and handed the overcoat to him. "Stay calm, buddy."

"What about the poker game?" Boomer was bemoaning.

\* \* \*

Kayla was about to knock on Jack's door when it was abruptly yanked open by a young black man wearing a Chicago Fire Department T-shirt. He almost ran her over in his hurry to depart.

"Whoa, where's the fire?" Kayla joked as she juggled Ashley on her hip. The smell of cigar smoke inside the apartment had her waving her free hand in front of her face and wrinkling her nose.

Ashley mimicked her mom's wrinkled nose and added a "Yucky!" to boot.

At the same time, an older man near the window he'd just opened a bit was saying, "Hey, it really *is* snowing out there! I think we better get out of here while the getting is good."

"What are you doing out in such bad weather?" Jack asked Kayla without getting up from his seat at the card table.

Kayla sighed. He didn't look pleased to see her. It seemed she'd walked in on a poker game or something. "The weather service has had a snow advisory every other week since Christmas," she said. "How was I supposed to know that this time they'd finally be right?"

"Hey, aren't you going to introduce us, buddy?" Boomer asked hopefully.

"Sure. Boomer, Sam...this is Kayla White and her daughter."

Jack frowned at the way Boomer fawned over Kayla while Sam charmed Ashley. The little girl even left the safety of her mother's arms to laugh at Sam's impersonation of a teddy bear.

Jack watched Ashley. The first and only time he'd seen her, she'd been just a kid. Now she was *Kayla's* kid.

He saw the resemblance, the same baby blue eyes full

of life. Ashley's hair was more red than brown and she had plenty of freckles on her little nose.

Looking at Kayla, he noticed the way the overhead light in his hallway was shining down on her hair, highlighting the occasional streak of red in the otherwise quiet brown. The fire hidden beneath the surface, that was Kayla, all right. At first she might seem haughty and stand-offish, but beneath those classy features and prim exterior lurked the heart of a passionate woman.

He'd felt her heart beating when he'd kissed her. He'd tasted that passion and found it addictive. He'd never kissed such luscious lips. Lips that his buddies were looking at much too intently.

"Weren't you guys leaving?" Jack reminded Sam and Boomer.

"That wasn't very hospitable of you," Kayla chastised him once the two men had gone.

"Yeah, well I'm not exactly known for being hospitable."

"I's not goin' to a hospitable," Ashley declared with a nervous look in Jack's direction. "They got big needles there."

"Tell me about it," Jack agreed. To Kayla he said, "You still haven't told me what you're doing out in this weather?"

"It wasn't that bad when we started out," she said defensively. "This is our last stop. I thought we'd be here earlier, but Ashley had a dance recital this afternoon and that ran long, and then the snow delayed us...but your place is on our way home, anyway. I just stopped to give you your groceries. There isn't much food in the refrigerator, in case you hadn't noticed."

"The guys brought food with them for the poker game."

"You didn't tell me that."

"I don't see any groceries."

Kayla looked down before flushing. "I must have left them in the hallway." Opening the door, she grabbed the plastic bag and carried it to the kitchen, with Ashley sticking to her like a spooked shadow. With quick efficiency Kayla put away the perishables and had the bag folded in less than a minute. "Now that that's done, we'll get out of your hair."

Jack blocked her way to the front door, crutches and all. "If you think I'm going to let you out again in this weather," he growled, "you're crazy."

# Four

---

"**I**'m not the one who's crazy," Kayla said.

"No?" Jack impatiently jerked his head toward the living room window, which was now open a crack to air out the place, thanks to Sam and Boomer's smoking. "Take a look outside."

Kayla did, in time to look down and see a cab nearly slide into the back end of a stopped bus on the slippery, snow-covered street. The near miss shook her, as did the rapidness with which the snow was falling—blowing sideways in a wind that was definitely picking up. She couldn't even see across the courtyard of Jack's apartment building.

Smoothing her daughter's hair back from her forehead, Kayla smiled down at her reassuringly before speaking to Jack. "So what are you suggesting? That we should stay here?"

"Is that such a wild idea?" Jack countered. "The couch turns into a pullout bed. You and your daughter can sleep out here in the living room. You didn't double-park out front again, did you?''

"No. I learn from past mistakes," she informed him with double meaning.

"It would definitely be a mistake to go back out in that."

Kayla bit her lip and murmured, "I don't know...."

"I *do*," he stated. "You're staying. That's final."

She narrowed her eyes at him in a look that Ashley could have told him meant trouble. "I don't respond well to orders."

"Neither do I." Far from being abashed by her reprimand, Jack actually had the nerve to smile at her. It was one of those wickedly knightly smiles of his. "But you've ordered me around plenty. Now you know how I feel."

Ah, but Kayla *didn't* always know how he felt—about a lot of things, including her. She couldn't tell if the flashes of hunger she saw darkening his turbulent eyes was his reaction to every woman who crossed his path—or if it was her. But why would a man like him, who could have any woman he wanted, be interested in a woman like her, a working mom who was nothing special to look at? And if he *was*, what did she plan on doing about it?

"Mommy, you said we wasn't staying long," Ashley stated. "Hugs wants to go home now."

"I know he does, sweetie. But you see how hard it's snowing outside? I think it would be safer if we stayed here."

"I wanna go home."

"You like pizza?" Jack suddenly asked Ashley. "I've got a pizza on its way up here anytime now. A big one." After all, Jack had thought he'd be sharing it with three guys who had the appetite of six. "And I've got cable TV—I bet there's something good on for kids...someplace." He sank onto the couch and reached for the remote with the air of a man grasping at a life vest.

Fate took pity on him, for Jack quickly found a channel geared for children, and it featured a cartoon that was one of Ashley's favorites, distracting her enough to allow Kayla to remove the little girl's coat and boots without her kicking up a fuss. But she stuck to her mom like glue, even following her to the window to close it.

Things proceeded smoother than he could have hoped, with the pizza arriving soon thereafter. The carton of chocolate mint ice cream he had in the freezer was a big hit with Ashley and lulled him into a false sense of security.

A quick switch to the weather channel confirmed that all of northern Illinois was under a winter storm warning, with upward of ten inches expected. Seven inches had already fallen, and the winds of over forty miles an hour had created white-out conditions across the Chicago area.

Ashley didn't set up a fuss again until it was time for her to go to bed. She clutched her mother with one hand and her teddy bear with the other. "I don' wanna stay here no more," she declared in no uncertain terms as only a three-year-old can. "I wanna go home. *Now!*"

"We can't, sweetie. There's too much snow. It's safer if we stay here, just for tonight. Then we'll go home tomorrow and play in all the snow in our front yard. We'll make a snowman, you'd like that, wouldn't you? Hugs can help."

"Hugs don' wanna help. We wanna go home."

"We can't go home," Kayla said in exasperation. "We have to stay here."

"Don' want to. I wanna go home," Ashley wailed. Pointing at Jack, she added, "He's the monster man!"

Jack, who'd been wincing at the shrill tone of Ashley's

childish voice, suddenly looked as if he'd been viciously struck with a whip. A second later his face went blank.

"I'm so sorry," Kayla quickly apologized. "She didn't mean that."

But Jack didn't hear her. He was lost in his own personal torment as the memories of another child who had thought him a monster came rushing into his mind.

It had happened his first year in the department, and he'd been trying to forget it ever since. Most days he was successful, although there were some at the firehouse who said that that single incident still governed Jack's actions ten years later. But they never talked to him about it, he made sure of that. Because no amount of talking could make the horrible reality go away.

He had to get out of here. Pivoting sharply, Jack left the room without saying a word.

Even Ashley was aware of the abrupt difference in Jack. She'd stopped crying and started sucking her thumb instead, something she did when uncertain or nervous.

"Ashley, you shouldn't have said that to Jack," Kayla reprimanded her. "Would you like someone saying that to you?"

The little girl removed her thumb long enough to mumble, "I's not mean."

"You don't think it's mean to call someone a monster? Would a monster share his pizza with you? Jack isn't mean, honey. You remember, when I read you that story about fire and not playing with matches, I told you that Jack is a fireman. He saves people."

"He didn't save us."

"Because we don't need saving. We scared him that first day we came, that's the only reason why he shouted at us then."

"He was scared of us?" The concept seemed to fascinate Ashley.

"That's right."

"How come?"

"Because he didn't know we were coming. Remember, I told you all this before?"

"Can't we go home?"

"No."

Ashley sucked her thumb for a few minutes and eyed her mother warily as Kayla made up the bed with the sheets Jack had brought out earlier. Then, nodding her head and tightening her hold on Hugs, Ashley made up her mind. She would fix the monster man just like in *Beauty and the Beast*.

At first the soft little voice didn't break through the darkness of Jack's memories. He'd been that wrapped up in the horror that he'd lost track of his surroundings. To his astonishment, Ashley was standing nearby, only a few feet from where he sat at the kitchen table. She was nervously running her left foot against the back of her right leg and tugging on the seat of her corduroy pants as she repeated her earlier words. "Is you sad?"

Jack didn't answer. He couldn't.

But Ashley proved to be as stubborn as her mother. "Did I make you sad?" she persisted.

Jack didn't know what to say.

But Ashley did. "I's sorry." With a shyly uncertain little smile that reminded him of Kayla, Ashley held out her teddy bear and said, "You wanna hug Hugs? Hugs make boomies better."

"Boomies?" Jack repeated, his voice rusty, as if his lungs had been burned by smoke.

"Boomies. When you hurt or is sad," Ashley explained.

"Hugs from Mommy are best, but Hugs is good, too. Aren't you gonna hug him?"

Jack looked to Kayla, who was standing in the kitchen doorway, for guidance. She just smiled.

"A hug from your mommy would be better," Jack murmured. Seeing the way the little girl's expression fell, he hastily added, "But teddy bears are nice."

"Hugs has *magic*," Ashley informed him.

"I can tell that," Jack said

When he continued to hesitate, Ashley asked, "Don' you know how to hug?"

"It's been a while since I hugged a teddy bear," Jack gruffly admitted.

"Want me to show you how?" the little girl offered.

"Okay."

Ashley took the bear and, wrapping both arms around the bedraggled-looking stuffed animal, gave it a giant bear hug. "Now you," she said, handing the bear to Jack again.

Feeling rather idiotic, he nonetheless did his best to imitate her efforts.

"See, that wasn't so hard, was it?" Kayla noted, her voice warm with approval.

It was harder than she thought. And so was he, Jack silently noted. Hardened by the realities of life, by the fact that he'd lost his faith in miracles when he'd lost his parents in that car accident. He loved fighting fire because he was good at it and he could make a difference, could save lives. Sometimes.

But it was the failures that haunted him at night, one failure in particular.

What would Kayla think of him if she knew about the darkness within him? Would she still smile at him or would she take her daughter and run? Why did he care so much? But care he did.

* * *

"She's finally asleep," Kayla whispered as she returned to the kitchen an hour later. "I'm sorry about what she said earlier. She was tired and crabby about not getting her way."

"You don't have to make excuses."

"I'm not. Well, maybe I am," she ruefully admitted. "I just…" How could she explain that she'd hated seeing that stricken look on his face, that haunted look in his gray eyes? "I'm sorry it happened."

He shrugged. "I told you I wasn't any good with kids."

"That had nothing to do with it. Swinging your crutch at us that first day is what scared Ashley. And that hug you gave Hugs was a big hit with her."

"Yeah, right."

"It was," Kayla insisted.

"So I did *one* thing right."

Kayla didn't know what had happened, but something else was going on here. Jack wasn't the type of man to get upset by something said by a child. His ego was much too strong for that. "You want to talk about it?" she hesitantly asked him.

"About what?" he countered. "The one thing I did right?"

"No. About what made you look so…I don't know. Stricken, I guess. There was something else going on."

"Bad memories."

"Of what?"

"Don't worry about it. I've been called worse things in my life," he mockingly assured her.

"Maybe. But maybe none as devastating. Why is that?"

Jack had never been one to spill his guts and he certainly wasn't about to start now, although there was just the slightest urge to let down his guard for once and confide in her. He squelched it immediately.

Instead of confiding, he joked. It was his way. "Did I tell you I'm going in to the doctor's office on Tuesday for my twenty-thousand-mile tune-up on these crutches?"

To his relief, Kayla played along. "Twenty-thousand miles already, hmm? Gee, how time flies when you're having fun."

"As soon as I see the doc I plan on returning to work."

"How can you do that? Your leg will still be in a cast for another two weeks yet."

"I won't be on active duty, but I can push papers for a while. Besides, I'm a fast healer. I've been banged up enough times to know that."

"You've broken bones before?"

"Nothing major. Got a half-dozen stitches on my left arm a few years back." He proudly showed her the scar. "And a hot ember once fell down my collar and left its mark. Want to see?"

His teasing smile was leaving its mark on her, tempting her, tugging on her heart and making it skip with unspoken longing.

"No, thanks," she said, hoping to sound nonchalant but the breathlessness of her voice gave her away. "I...ah...I see you've added some more signatures to your cast?"

"Yeah, some of the guys from the station stopped by the other day, but you'd better not read what they wrote..."

His warning came too late. Kayla was already bent over his leg, her dainty hand on his knee as she tried to decipher what had been written. Jack was chagrined at some of the raunchy stuff the guys had put on there. He'd never dreamed that Kayla would read it.

"Your friends have an overactive imagination," was all she said. "Including the female ones with the flowery handwriting who put their mark on you."

"On my *cast,* not on me," Jack replied.

Kayla could see that. She had a feeling Jack didn't allow anyone to put their mark on him to touch his heart as well as his body. Not in a very long time.

But confronting him about it wouldn't accomplish anything, so she said, "That's a cute little happy face Sammi put over the *i* in her name."

"We're just friends," he maintained.

"You being the friendly sort and all that, right?" She grinned at his discomfiture.

"How did we get started on this subject?"

"You asked if I wanted to see your scars, a line that's no doubt worked well with the other women you've tried it on."

"You think I go walking down the street, asking strange women if they want to see my scars?"

"You wouldn't have to walk very far to get a yes." What had started as a thought somehow became the spoken words. Now it was Kayla's turn to squirm in discomfort.

"I wouldn't, huh? Nice to know, but the thing is that I'm not interested in any strange woman on the street. I'm interested in you."

"Meaning I'm a strange woman?"

"You're a beautiful woman."

She rolled her eyes. "Now I *know* you're full of hot air."

"What, you think you're not beautiful?"

"I *know* I'm not."

"You've never heard that beauty is in the eye of the beholder?"

"I've heard it, I just don't believe it."

"What do you believe in?"

"My daughter."

"And is she the only thing that makes you happy?"

"Not the only thing, no. But the most important thing. What about you? What makes *you* happy?"

"Embarrassing you," he promptly replied with a naughty grin.

She laughed. "If that were true, then your face wouldn't have turned red when I was reading the words on your cast."

"My face did not turn red," he denied. "I was hot."

"I would have thought a firefighter would be used to heat."

"Not the kind you make me feel."

His quiet admission dazzled her. Their eyes met. His smoky gaze locked on to hers and pulled her in with the promise of forbidden pleasure. Logical thought skittered away, replaced by a visual communication that evoked images of satin sheets and naked bodies. His. Hers. Entwined together in search of satisfaction…and finding it.

She had to say something to break this expectant silence. What had they been talking about before? His job. "Umm…" She had to pause in order to clear her throat and her thoughts. "Did you always want to be a firefighter?"

"Yeah, I guess so. I didn't adjust well to most of the foster homes I was in, but when I got to my adopted parents' place I was impressed by the fact that Sean was a firefighter. I used to dog him all the time, following him around and asking him questions. It's a wonder he didn't toss me out on my butt. But he was always patient and he told the greatest stories—still does, now that he's retired. He's a real 'smoke eater,' an old-timer."

"So you wanted to be a firefighter because of your adopted father?"

"It started earlier than that."

Something in his voice made her say, "If you don't want to talk about it…"

Jack shrugged and took a sip of his imported ale before speaking. "I told you my parents died in a car accident. It was a head-on collision. I was in the car with them."

"Oh, Jack…"

He cut through her sympathy like a knife. "The firefighters on the scene had to use the Jaws of Life to get them out. They tried to save them, but…" His voice trailed off, and he shrugged and took another drink before continuing. "Still, I was impressed by their, I don't know, their bravery I guess." Another shrug. "Even now, after all these years, I still hate it when we're called in to a car accident and we have to use the Jaws."

"That's understandable."

"Yeah, well…" He shifted in the plastic kitchen chair, clearly uncomfortable with what he'd said. "I didn't mean to get so sappy about stuff."

"You weren't. I'm glad you told me." It was yet another piece in the complicated puzzle that was Jack Elliott.

"Are you feeling better about staying here tonight?" he asked her.

"I guess so. I mean, it's not as if we were planning on fooling around all night or anything," Kayla began nervously.

Jack interrupted her to teasingly say, "Not *all* night maybe."

She wrinkled her nose at him as embarrassment colored her cheeks. "I put that badly."

"You don't do anything badly…not that I can think of."

"You don't know me that well."

"Not yet, but I hope to."

"We'll have to see about that."

Their eyes met again, but this time Kayla knew better

than to allow herself get caught up in the magic of his gaze. "Tell me more about the work you do."

"I fight fires."

"I gathered that much," she said in exasperation. "What do they do with a firefighter who's broken his leg?"

"Shoot him and put him out of his misery," Jack retorted.

She laughed.

Jack smiled. He loved the sound of her laughter. It was so...he didn't know how to describe it. Full of life. Heartwarming. Husky. Sexy. All that and more.

"You miss it, don't you." Her softly spoken words were more observation than question.

"Yeah, I do."

"Tell me more about your work. What's a normal day like?"

"There is no such thing." Seeing that she wasn't going to accept that answer, he went on to add, "But I can give you a rough idea. I'm on duty twenty-four hours then off for forty-eight. My shift begins at 8:00 a.m. and includes physical training like weight lifting...."

That explained his magnificent chest, Kayla thought to herself.

"But no training on how to get around on these," he grumbled with a mocking look at his crutches.

"You're doing better at that," she said.

"Maybe. Anyway, like I said, a day is never normal because we drop everything whenever we get a call, and you don't know when or how often that will be. We respond to fires, gas leaks, chemical spills, medical emergencies, all kinds of stuff. When we're not doing that, we're doing drills or checking and maintaining the equipment and vehicles. You know, siren, lights, fuel, oxygen, air pressure in the SCBA..."

"The what?"

"Self-contained breathing apparatus. You need to make sure the masks are clean and the regulators functioning. Basically you're trying to make sure everything is ready to go, that's why you check and recheck."

She nodded her understanding and looked at him expectantly, clearly waiting to hear more.

"Lunch is at noon, and we take turns doing the cooking and cleaning up, every shift does its own. There are floors to be washed, axes to be sharpened, hoses to be rolled and tested. And then there's plenty of brass to be polished. I'm a pro at polishing," Jack noted, giving her a devilish head-to-toe look. "You have anything that needs polishing or rubbing, I'm your man."

"I'll keep that in mind," she replied, her voice on the breathless side due to the steamy images he'd just conjured up, polishing and rubbing her skin instead of brass.

"Yeah, well like I said, we do a lot of training, drilling on ladders, working with saws, smoke ejectors, extinguishers or other equipment, tying knots backward and forward, with our eyes closed if need be. I'm also a pro with knots."

"Knots? What are those for?"

"We use rope to move people and equipment. And when you use rope you've got to have special knots."

Which sounded very plain and practical. So why, Kayla wondered, did she get this sudden erotic image of Jack using silken ropes and special knots to bind her to a brass headboard draped like a decadent harem? Blinking away her heated fantasy, she tried to refocus her attention on what he was saying.

"We study firefighting manuals, preplan attack strategies for various buildings and classes of fire. This comes in mighty handy, because if you're fighting a Class C fire you better know that means an electrical fire. If the electricity is still on and you try dousing it with water, you could end up electrocuting yourself. So it's a good idea to pay attention to these things. It's not a job for wimps. My boots alone weigh ten pounds and by the time I'm in full gear I'm dragging around eighty-some pounds of equipment with me into a burning building most sane people would be running *out* of, not into.''

"So why do you do it?"

"I never claimed to be sane."

There he was again, she silently noted, using humor to wiggle out of answering.

"I didn't mean to drone on and on about my work like that," he noted wryly. "But sometimes the public thinks we do nothing but sit around the firehouse all day goofing off.''

"You didn't drone on and on," Kayla said. "I liked hearing about it." She also just plain liked the sound of his voice. He'd never talked for such an extended period before. It was clear to her how much he loved his work, how much he missed it while he was recovering. "Tell me more."

"There's not much more to tell except that in my book, high-rise fires are the worst. You never know what you're getting into and it's a hell of a job getting back out. This building only has four stories, and you notice I'm on the second floor. That's because I hate high-rises."

"Me, too," she agreed. "I just never felt comfortable so far from the front door."

"So you don't live in a high-rise, then?"

"No. I'm renting a small house at the moment." But it was just that—a house, not a home. Oh, she'd fixed up Ashley's room so that it was any little girl's dream, and the rest of the place was clean and orderly, but just not *home*. It was just someplace to stay until she could find something better.

"At the moment?" Jack repeated.

"Someday I'd like a place of my own," Kayla wistfully confessed. "Bruce and I were living in an apartment near the hospital when we got divorced and that's when I moved to this house three years ago. It's very small, but that makes it easy to clean. I sure wish it had more closet space, though," she muttered. Looking around the big kitchen, she added, "This building seems nice."

The brick building was in the shape of a *U* with a center courtyard that someone had had the foresight to plant a few evergreens in years ago. Since Jack was in an end unit, he had windows in both the living room and the kitchen.

"You're lucky to have a window over your kitchen sink," she noted. Her house didn't have that, so she'd been forced to put a poster there or go nuts from staring at a blank wall while doing the dishes. "At least you've got a view of sorts."

"Yeah," Jack agreed, "you can see across the courtyard to the apartment over there. Last summer, there were some female college exchange students from Sweden living there and the guys brought over binoculars—"

"You spied on them with binoculars?"

"I wasn't spying."

"What were you doing? Trying to read the name brand on their smoke detectors?"

He grinned. "I'll have to try that line sometime."

She shook her head at his clearly unrepentant expression. "Someday, some woman is going to bring you to your knees and make you sorry for all the stuff you've done to the female gender over the years. I just hope I'm around to see it."

"You might not just be around," Jack replied in a husky voice. "You might be the woman to do it."

"Oh no, it would take a braver woman than me."

"You don't seem like the faint-hearted kind to me."

"As I said before, you don't know me very well."

"Yet," he reminded her. "Look at all the things I've learned tonight."

"And what have you learned tonight?"

"That you hog all the mushrooms on a pizza while avoiding the green peppers."

"I did not hog the mushrooms!" Kayla protested.

"And you aim your pinkie in the air like a duchess or something when you're drinking, even if it's from the bottle."

"You don't have any decent glasses."

"Don't have any indecent ones left, either. I got a set for Christmas from Sam, shaped like a woman's...ah, maybe I'd better not share that story."

"Maybe you'd better not," she agreed before adding, "Sam and your other friends seemed very nice."

"The guys are great. We've worked together for a long time now. We work the same shift, and spend time together all in one place, sleeping, eating, drilling... Well, all I can say is that it lets you see the true character of a guy. It's more than team spirit, more than a buddy system. We count on each other, watch each other's backs and save each other's hides. Day in, day out. If I ever get in trouble, they're there for me. And I'm there for them. No matter what happens, I know I can depend on them."

His quiet words touched her deeply. "And here I was thinking you were the kind to avoid commitment. But it sounds as if you and your friends are very committed to each other."

"I've often said we should be committed," was Jack's teasing reply. "To the funny farm."

She refused to let him off the hook. She knew Jack well enough to know that he used humor to wiggle out of any possibly emotional situation. "You don't think that kind of commitment, your being able to depend on someone, can happen outside the firehouse?"

"Sure it happens, I guess. Aside from my adoptive parents, it never has happened to me. Besides, that kind of commitment, the emotional kind, can eat a man alive. That wasn't what I was talking about."

She had her answer. It didn't make her happy, though.

Needing a distraction, she got up to get a can of soda from the fridge. It was down on the bottom shelf so she had to bend and reach way into the back to get it. Once she had the soda in hand, she straightened and bumped into Jack, who'd stood to join her...or seduce her.

She could read the look in his eyes as clearly as a headline. He definitely had seduction on his mind.

The refrigerator door closed behind her, and she scooted backward, away from the temptation of his smiling mouth.

The man was on crutches, she reminded herself, what could he do? She soon found out.

# Five

This time Jack didn't make his move suddenly. Instead he took things very slowly, heightening her awareness of what was to come. She was vaguely aware of him bracing one of his crutches against the kitchen counter. Then he removed the soda can from her right hand.

She was prepared for him to kiss her, had all her defenses in place, when he shattered them by lifting her hand and kissing it instead of her mouth, nibbling on her trembling fingers as if she were the greatest delicacy. His enticingly stealthy approach caught her by complete surprise.

Kayla shivered with pleasure at the delicate touch of his tongue on the ultrasensitive web of skin between her thumb and index finger. She could feel the texture of his lips, the slight abrasion of his unshaven skin. Parting her lips in anticipation, she breathlessly waited to see what he'd do next.

Separating her index finger from the others, he leisurely

drew her fingertip into his mouth, laving the tender pad with the very tip of his tongue. More shock waves of delight hit her nervous system when he moved her finger from his mouth to hers. She could taste him on her skin.

Kayla was stunned by how incredibly erotic the gesture was. *There are plenty of times when slower is better,* he'd once told her. Now she knew what he meant. The buildup was incredible!

Warm puffs of his breath ricocheted off her cheek as he leaned closer. But still he didn't kiss her lips. Instead he brushed his mouth across her cheek before honing in on her ear, lifting her hair out of his way and nuzzling his way into new territory.

Kayla got goose bumps. She *never* got goose bumps, unless it was below zero outside. But it was the heat, not the cold that was getting to her now. The heat radiating from his body to hers, and the fire he was spreading with his masterful touch.

Spearing his fingers through her hair, he swirled his tongue around the shell-like curve of her ear.

Had that breathless little gasp come from her? Yes. She couldn't help it, she gasped again as she was bombarded with sensations created by the slow seduction of his caressing hand, the warmth of his mouth, the feel of his beating heart beneath her hand—a hand she'd put out to draw him even closer.

The refrigerator was at her back, humming against her. Radiant excitement was humming through her system, thrumming through her bloodstream, pumping into her heart.

Kayla's eyes drifted shut. Now she was even more dependent on her other senses, aware of the tiniest thing like the rapid cadence of her breathing and his. His mouth oh, so slowly, drifted over her cheek to the corner of her lips.

Her heart was racing and her knees were shaking and Jack had yet to kiss her.

The anticipation was at a fever pitch. She could feel him near, could almost taste him.

Kayla opened her eyes to see what was making him wait. He was so close she couldn't focus on him. But she could focus on his lips.

"Beautiful," he whispered against her mouth, tasting and testing the fullness of her lower lip.

Her breath caught at the seductive action. He captured her tiny moan of pleasure and incorporated it into their kiss, covering her parted lips with his at long last. Dipping his tongue into the warm depths of her mouth, he displayed a sensual creativity that made her knees even weaker.

She leaned against the fridge, Jack leaned against her. She was tightly sandwiched between the humming appliance at her back and Jack's throbbing arousal at her front.

Making good use of his one free hand, Jack shifted his hold on her, sliding his splayed fingers into her hair and bracing his palm at her nape, preparing her for the increasing intensity of his kiss. This had been worth waiting for. This was total consumption, total absorption, total elation.

The electrifying thrust of his hips was darkly tempting. She was on fire, blindly compelled by passion to meet the driving motion of his mouth and body with the same heated urgency until she lost all track of time and place.

Suddenly the refrigerator made a giant nose, shuddering as if it were in the midst of a death throe and startling her.

"What was that?" she shakenly asked.

"The refrigerator," he muttered against her mouth. "Ignore it."

But Kayla couldn't do that. Now that she'd been literally jarred out of her sensual haze, reality had taken hold. What had she been thinking of? Her daughter was asleep in the other room. What kind of mother was she to be making out in the kitchen with a man like Jack?

A sexy, passionate, incredible man like Jack, a wayward corner of her mind whispered. Her ex-husband paled in comparison to Jack. Bruce may have been good-looking and outwardly happy-go-lucky, but underneath that slick exterior was a man devoid of true emotion, self-serving and lacking real passion unless it concerned his work. Caring only for himself. Not caring for her or her daughter, unless it suited him.

The memory gave her strength. "Let me go."

Sighing and muttering under his breath, Jack reluctantly loosened his hold on her before deftly grabbing the one crutch he'd set aside. "We do seem to be making a habit of this," he grumbled in a voice rough with male aggravation. "Of having appliances interrupting us making out. First Ernie on the intercom and now this."

"It has to stop."

"I agree," he murmured, fighting the powerful urge to take her in his arms again. If it weren't for his stupid broken leg, he'd sweep her in arms and carry her to his bed where he'd make love to her until daylight. "Next time, we won't let anything stop us...."

"No, I mean the kissing. It has to stop."

"Why?"

"Because."

Kayla's return to that prim tone of voice spurred his anger. "I'm not a three-year-old," he growled. "That answer's not gonna carry any weight with me. Because why? Because you liked it too much?"

"Yes."

Her honesty surprised him. "So what's wrong with that?"

"Everything. We're looking for different things. You want a quick roll in the hay and I want…"

"You want me," he inserted.

Her blue eyes flashed at him. "You're not the first man I've wanted."

"I never thought I was. I mean, you've got a daughter, after all. You were married. You must have felt something for the guy."

"I loved him with all my heart."

Kayla's words cut him unexpectedly, like a rope that slid through your hands if you weren't paying attention. "So what happened?"

"He was really good-looking, popular with women. Like you."

Jack wanted to shout that he was nothing like her ex-husband.

"We met in college. My first week there, in fact. I was so surprised that he paid any attention to me, that he asked me out."

"Why should that surprise you? I told you before, you're a beautiful woman."

"I am not. I was dumpy in high school and even that first year in college. Definitely what you'd call a late bloomer, if I bloomed at all."

"Oh, you've bloomed, all right," he growled, tugging her to him and running his thumb over her nipple. Her blue knit top amplified the raw power of his caress.

"Stop playing games with me," she said.

Deciding that actions spoke louder than words, he grabbed her hand and placed it over the placket of his jeans. "Does this feel like I'm playing games? Lady, I'm dead serious here."

She hurriedly snatched her hand away, more because she was tempted to keep it where it was than out of any sense of outrage. "I already told you, I'm not interested in a one-night stand."

"It's gonna take more than one night for the fire between us to burn out," Jack replied in a sexy whisper. "Trust me, I'm an expert at these things."

He'd meant he was an expert with fire, but she took him to mean with affairs. "I know you're an expert, you've done this lots of times before, had lots of women."

"Not all that many," he muttered. "I'm healthy, if that's what you're asking. I just gave blood at the firehouse last month...."

"That's not what I was asking."

"Well, you should. It's a dangerous world out there."

"And you're making it a more dangerous one."

Her accusation stung. "How do you figure that?"

"Because I've seen the pattern before."

"I'm not like you're ex-husband." There—he'd said the words. Growled them, actually.

"He was happy-go-lucky like you."

Offended, Jack muttered, "I am *not* happy-go-lucky."

"We were happy at first," Kayla said, ignoring Jack's comment. "At least I like to think we were. *I* was happy. Even though I was working long hours and we didn't see enough of each other."

"Why was that?"

"Because Bruce was studying. He was in medical school. I worked to help out."

"You mean you paid his way?"

"He had a scholarship that helped out some."

"Some? The guy sounds like a no-good moocher to me."

"I found that out when he divorced me, after he finished his internship. He'd met someone else. Someone from a wealthy Oak Brook family. She had the background he'd always wanted. So he left.''

"He left his wife and kid for some rich chick from the suburbs?"

"Yeah, go figure," she said on the edge of a sob.

"If there weren't a kid in the other room, I'd give you a few choice words to describe the bastard you married."

"If there weren't a child in the other room, we wouldn't be having this conversation. But Ashley is the most important thing in my life, and I'm not going to let anything threaten her well-being."

Jack's smoky eyes turned bleak.

"I don't mean that you're a threat to her," Kayla quickly clarified. "I don't mean that at all. I mean that getting involved with you would give my ex-husband the ammunition he needs to get custody of Ashley."

"He wants custody?"

"He's talked about it. They've recently found out that his new wife can't have children of her own."

"So she wants yours?"

His words were very similar to the ones Kayla had used a few weeks ago.

"Is your ex-husband threatening you?" Jack demanded.

"He's talked about taking Ashley."

"What does your attorney say? Surely no court would give a kid to the man who deserted his wife and baby. Ashley must have been just a baby when this happened."

Kayla nodded. "She was only a few months old. Her crying prevented Bruce from getting enough sleep. He used to complain bitterly about that. A surgeon needs his sleep, he'd tell me over and over again."

"And what? Now that she's past that stage, she's convenient to have around again? Is that it?"

"I don't know what Bruce is thinking," Kayla wearily

admitted. "But I do know that he'd use anything he could against me. So there's no way I can get...involved with anyone at this point in my life."

"So what do you plan on doing? Keeping your sex life on hold until your daughter is eighteen? You're a passionate woman. You need a man—"

She angrily interrupted him. "If I *did* need a man, it would be one who was willing to..."

"Go on," he taunted her. "Willing to what?"

"Willing to commit. A man who is looking for more than a fleeting affair. A man who's looking for forever. Is that what you're looking for?" she challenged him.

The answer was in his eyes and his silence.

"I didn't think so," she whispered.

"I don't believe in forever anymore. But if I did..."

It didn't matter. Kayla wasn't there to hear his words any longer. She'd gone to bed; to her daughter and her commitments. Without him.

Jack woke the next morning with the strangest feeling that someone was looking at him. And it sure did feel like someone was sitting on him.

His eyes popped open to find Ashley perched on his bed, her knees pinning down the blankets by his side and thus pinning him to the bed. At least she wasn't sitting on top of him. Instead she was leaning over him and staring at him about four inches from his chin.

Startled, the only reason Jack didn't jump out of his skin and his bed was the fact that he didn't want to scare Ashley. Not knowing quite what to say, Jack decided to let the kid talk first. She took her own sweet time about it.

"I was making sure you wasn't dead," she told him. Pointing to his bare chest, she added, "You got hair like Hugs does."

Disconcerted, Jack tugged the white sheet up to his throat, nearly dislodging Ashley from her princesslike perch in the process.

"Hugs is hungry. He wants choclotts. Now."

"I don't have any chocolate."

"Uh-oh," Ashley said.

"Uh-oh, what?" Jack asked suspiciously, his panicked thoughts skittering from one kid-induced disaster to another. Surely Ashley was toilet trained by now, right? She wasn't going to wet on his bed or anything was she? Just because he didn't have chocolate?

"Uh-oh my mommy is coming," Ashley said. Leaning closer to Jack, she confided, "She's gonna be mad."

"Oh? Why's that?"

"She said don't wake you. But I didn't. Hugs did. Hi, Mommy!" she said with a brilliant smile aimed at Kayla.

"Hi, yourself, sprite. I thought I told you not to bother Jack."

"I wasn't. His eyes opened. He doesn't have choclotts, Mommy."

"I thought we'd have pancakes for breakfast." Coming to his bed, Kayla leaned to talk to Ashley. Kayla's movement let Jack see the curve of her breast displayed by the V-necked Wildcats T-shirt he'd lent her to sleep in last night.

The hem went down to her knees and was actually longer than her skirts were. But there was something about seeing her in his clothing that made him want to see her in nothing at all. And then there was the fact that she was in his bedroom. And she was surreptitiously looking around with more than casual interest.

"Looking for mirrors and a round vibrating bed, are you?" he mocked her.

"No. I was just thinking how neat you've got things in here."

"I told you I'm not a total slob."

Unwilling to risk the danger of feasting her eyes on him, she let her gaze wander to the window. "I looked out the living room window and there seems to be almost a foot of snow outside."

Afraid she was getting ready to leave, Jack said, "You better give the snow plows more time to work on the streets. I've got a buddy in Streets and Sanitation who usually makes sure my street gets cleared by noon."

"Are we gonna eat now?" Ashley demanded.

"You've got a one-track mind," Kayla said, even as she grabbed the little girl around the middle and nuzzled her neck until she giggled. "No more roughhousing on Jack's bed, he's got a broken leg. Come on, you, I'll see if I can't rustle up some pancakes for us to eat."

After the two had left, Jack stayed in bed, mesmerized by the image of Kayla on his bed. She'd looked good there, her hair falling into her eyes, the oversize T-shirt slipping off one shoulder. So good that he had to take a cold shower before making an idiot of himself.

His mood hadn't improved by the time he was done. He'd been in such an all-fire hurry that he'd left his clothes in his bedroom. When he yanked open the bathroom door, which had an irritating habit of sticking with humidity, he was muttering under his breath and praying the towel he'd fastened around his waist would stay put while he used the crutches to propel himself as fast as humanly possible into his bedroom.

To his relief, Ashley was in the living room, watching Saturday morning cartoons. Kayla was a heck of a lot closer, as in only a few feet away.

Jack's glare was enough to melt steel, but Kayla paid it

no heed. History was repeating itself. She'd kept that memory of him coming out of the shower in her head even though it had happened days before. But her fantasies didn't hold a candle to reality. Reality was *so* much better!

She'd felt his chest pressed against her breasts last night; she knew how solid it was. She'd forgotten how darn good it looked. And his shoulders. And everything else in between...and below....

"Don't look at me like that unless you mean it," Jack warned her in a gravelly voice.

Refusing to back down, she took pleasure in the fact that he sounded as rattled as she'd felt when she'd first seen him step out of the bathroom. But it wouldn't do to let him know that. So she calmly said, "Listen, I'm a mother. You don't intimidate me. I've seen it all."

"Not yet you haven't. But if you keep standing there in my bedroom doorway any longer, you will." As if to reinforce his statement, the towel around his waist slipped another inch.

"I'm moving, I'm moving!" she hurriedly declared, her earlier calm completely deserting her.

As he swept past her on his crutches, she could feel the heat radiating from him. Then the bedroom door slammed in her face.

By Monday the city, while still digging out, had mostly returned to normal. But Kayla hadn't returned to normal. Her friend Diane knew something was up when Kayla dropped by the office.

"That was some snowstorm, huh?" Diane said as the Beatles' *Abbey Road* compact disk quietly played from the corner of the office.

"Yeah."

"You never did tell me where you and Ashley crashed

that first night,'' Diane noted while watering her collection of Boston ferns. Diane had called, over the weekend, to make sure Kayla was okay, but hadn't heard any details.

"We had to stay over at Jack's.''

"Jack Elliott? Now this sounds interesting. Not that you've told me much. Yet.''

"There's nothing to tell. We slept on the pullout in the living room. Ashley and I, I mean.''

"I figured that much. And nothing happened between you and Jack? Aha, you're blushing.''

Kayla sighed. "You should see the man, Diane. I wouldn't be human if I weren't...''

"Yes?''

"Affected by him.''

"He kissed you again, didn't he?'' Diane guessed. "And you liked it even more this time. The look on your face says it all.''

"I'm not getting involved with him. I'm not,'' Kayla stated emphatically. "I told him so.''

"What did he say?''

"He as much as admitted he's not a forever kind of guy. I made a mistake with Bruce, I'm not about to do that again.''

"Speaking of the no-good swine, have you heard from your ex-husband lately?''

"No, but he's supposed to come by next weekend to pick up Ashley. I know it's good for her to have time with her father, even if he was a jerk as a husband, but I miss her so much when she's gone. And lately I've got this almost overwhelming fear that Bruce won't bring her back.''

"He wouldn't risk his position in the medical community by having the police show up at his door. Bruce is stupid, but not that stupid.''

"Yeah, you're right." She deliberately shoved aside her dark thoughts. "Well, enough of this girl talk, we've got work to do."

"Look on the bright side," Diane pointed out. "At least you don't have to take the Newlins' toy poodle Puffkins for her grooming appointment like I do."

"If you had a name like Puffkins, you'd have an attitude problem, too," Kayla said as she printed up her daily schedule of the errands she had to run for clients today. The laser printer needed a new cartridge soon. Something else to add to the list. "Besides, I've got enough on my plate with the Bronkowski account."

"And Jack. Don't forget Jack."

"I don't visit Jack on Mondays."

"That doesn't mean you can forget about him, does it?"

"Believe me, I've tried," Kayla muttered. "Unfortunately it doesn't work. He's unforgettable."

"The offer to take over his account still stands," Diane told her with a grin. "Compared to Puffkins, the guy would be a piece of cake."

"You're making that up," Kayla told Jack, wiping the tears of laughter from her eyes and hoping her mascara was as waterproof as it had promised. She'd made her scheduled stop at his place on Tuesday, prepared for a confrontation. Instead he'd regaled her with stories and tall tales, or in this case tall tails.

"I'm telling you the dog did it. Clever mutt pulled the emergency fire alarm twice in that building. Just stood on its haunches and tugged the handle in its mouth. And then had the nerve to sit there until we arrived. The animal was as deaf as a stone, so the racket never bothered it."

"And you responded by…?"

"Taking the dog back to the firehouse. It was a stray,

anyway, and I figured that it just liked us, so I'd make it easier on him by bringing the dog to the firehouse instead of bringing the firehouse to the dog again.''

"And that's your story of how the firehouse went to the dogs.''

"That's right. You wouldn't believe some of the things we're called out on. Another one of my favorites happened during that sub-zero snap we had in December. We're called out to a car fire, the vehicle is completely engulfed when we get there. It turns out that the owner had put a sleeping bag on her car's engine to keep it warm. She kept it under the hood as she drove to work at a restaurant. She parked the car and left it, thinking everything is hunky-dory. It's not, because the sleeping bag ends up igniting. Next time she looks out the window of the restaurant she sees us there. She comes running out and so does the cook, who says 'So who ordered the Chevy well-done?' Now the moral of this story is that you put your girlfriend in your sleeping bag, not your car.''

The image of her and Jack cuddling together created a warmth that might well have set something ablaze.

As if reading her thoughts, Jack said, ''Are you ready to talk about that kiss?''

He caught her by surprise, but she hurriedly gathered her defenses in order to calmly say, ''What's left to talk about?''

"Plenty. There's something going on between us. I don't know what it is yet, but I want to find out.''

"I don't.''

"Why not? What are you afraid of?''

"I'm afraid of snakes and matches if they aren't the wooden safety variety.''

Her mocking reply got his attention. ''I've never heard of anyone being afraid of matches of any kind.''

"Well, *afraid* might be a strong way to describe it. I just can't strike any other kind of match to get them lit because I'm so afraid of getting burned that I drop it before it lights. But I work around it by using wooden matches. The wood doesn't bend like that cardboard paper stuff does."

Kayla didn't seem like the kind who would bend, either, Jack noted. She had her values and her rules and she stuck to them like glue. "I've never seen anyone make as many lists as you do," he noted as she crossed off something in her notebook.

"I like being organized."

"I *like* kissing you."

"Are we back to that?"

"Not yet, but I'd like to be."

"You're impossible."

"So you've told me."

What was it about the man that got to her so much? There had to be more to it than just his good looks and incredibly mind-bending kisses. He made her laugh as often as he made her furious.

"You're looking at me funny," he told her. "Are you trying to decide how to break my other leg?"

"You never told me the real story about how you broke the one you did break."

"Are you hungry? Want some lunch? I can order us a pizza."

Realizing he'd finagled his way out of talking about his injury yet again, she shook her head at both his maneuvering and his nutritional choices. "Do you live on pizza?"

"Not all the time, but it's handy having a pizzeria around the corner."

"I'm not hungry."

"You look hungry," he told her with a slow smile. "It's something about your eyes and the way you keep licking your lips as if you were dying to taste something...or someone."

"Taste or snap at someone," she retorted.

"Go right ahead," he invited her. "Give it your best shot, or best snap. I've felt those dainty teeth on me before, and I'd be happy to repeat the experience."

She blushed, remembering how passionately they'd kissed against the refrigerator door. "I already told you that experience will never be repeated."

"You've told me," he agreed as she walked out the front door. "You have yet to convince me."

The next night Jack called her at home to tell her that the doctor had given him the green light to go back to work. "I feel like celebrating, even if I am only going back to push papers for now. Maybe I'll torment the new probie with a pop quiz on combating hazmats."

"Hazmats?" she repeated. "Sounds like some kind of Eastern torture."

"Hazardous materials," he explained. "So when are you coming over?"

"What?"

"You and Ashley. I'm inviting you both over for dinner. I'm cooking. Irish stew." Jack added each sentence as if it were the next level of temptation. "Come on," he coaxed her. "What can happen with a three-year-old as a chaperon?"

"Plenty," she replied, remembering all too well what had happened the last time Ashley had been there. Granted, Ashley had been asleep in the other room when Jack had kissed Kayla until she'd been a heartbeat from surrendering. But still, Jack had proved to be dangerous to Kayla's self-control at a time when she would have thought she was temptation proof.

"Well, *plenty* won't happen this time," he assured her. "Unless you want it to."

"Why me?" Kayla asked. "I mean, why us? Why choose us to celebrate with?"

"Because you helped me get back on my feet, or as back on them as I am. You've got to admit I'm much more graceful on those stupid crutches now than I was in the beginning. You helped in my recovery, and I want to show my thanks. It's just dinner, Kayla. Not a lifetime commitment, okay?"

"Okay," she reluctantly agreed. He'd sounded so darn cheerful about wanting to celebrate with them, she didn't have the heart to turn him down. Not when he sounded that way so rarely. At least since she'd met him.

"Tell Ashley I got bear choclotts for Hugs," Jack said.

"They better be the invisible kind," Kayla replied.

"How did you know?"

"You catch on fast," she said, congratulating him.

"I like to think I do. So I'll see you here tomorrow night around five?"

"Okay."

To her relief, Kayla didn't have to convince Ashley to agree to go to Jack's place.

"Jack had a spell on him, but I fixed it," Ashley told her matter-of-factly.

"And how did you do that?"

"By being a princess. Jack was mean cause he was hurt. Just like 'Beauty and the Beast.' I want Belle's dress. I'll protect Jack. Can Hugs have choclotts now?"

Kayla grinned at the way her daughter's thoughts bounced around like a basketball in a Bulls game, first this way then that and finally way over there.

"Hugs helped fix Jack," Ashley added. "I won't call Jack a monster. No one else better be mean to him." She militantly stuck out her chin in a posture that Kayla recognized as her don't-mess-with-me stance. "Or else because." It was her own way of describing dire circumstances.

Kayla knew that her daughter had always been one to help an underdog. If there was a child in day care who got picked on by the others, that was the child that Ashley would take under her wing. The trait made Kayla so proud that she could only gaze at Ashley in wonder. How could this adorable little one have turned out so well from a marriage that had gone so bad? Kayla didn't know, she could only be grateful for the incredible and always surprising gift that was Ashley.

"What do three-year-olds eat?" Jack frantically asked Sam over the phone.

"Nervous guys," Sam retorted. "Would you just calm down?"

"They're going to be here in fifteen minutes."

"Your mom runs a day care center, why don't you ask her?"

"Because she's not home or I would have."

"Would this three-year-old be the same little redheaded one who stopped by your place with a cute looking mom during that last snowstorm?"

"Yeah, that's the one."

"And is she? Is this Kayla the *one* for you?"

"Why the inquisition?" Jack retorted in exasperation. "All I did was ask you a simple question, and you've practically got me hitched to the woman."

"I just hate to see a poor sap like you running around

loose, having a dozen busty women signing your cast, without a good woman to call your own.''

"I'm touched by your concern," Jack retorted with sarcasm.

"Yeah, you sound it." Sam laughed. "Just don't give her spinach or turnips. Three-year-olds hate spinach or turnips.''

Jack groaned. It was too late. He already had turnips in the stew. Maybe if he fed Ashley some mint ice cream in the beginning... He could see that going over really big with Kayla.

The buzzer rang just as he hung up the phone.

"Yeah?" Jack said after pushing the Speak button.

"This is Ernie, your doorman." He spoke with the speed of a centurion turtle.

"I know who you are, Ernie. What do you want? I'm busy.''

"You have two guests. A Ms. Kayla White and her daughter Miss Ashley White.''

"Kayla's been coming here for nearly three weeks, Ernie, and you've never once announced her. Why are you starting now?''

"Those were service calls," Ernie declared in his customary deadpan voice. "I always announce guests. I wanted your approval before sending them up.''

Jack was tempted to run downstairs, broken leg and all, and wring Ernie's thick neck. Instead he hung on to his temper and growled, "Send them up.''

Using the crutches, he propelled himself toward the front door like a pro. He was wearing a shirt and gray sweater along with the jeans that had one leg sliced open to accommodate his cast.

To Jack's surprise, Ashley was the first to greet him, and she did so by walking right up to him and hugging his good leg. "Tell my mommy how you's fixed now," she ordered him, blinking her baby blues at him.

"Fixed?" His wary gaze shot over to Kayla's laughing one.

"Fixed," Kayla agreed with a grin. "Not as in spayed, however."

"That's a relief."

"I'm a princess," Ashley declared with a little pirouette. "I fixed your bad spell. Hugs helped. Are you going to hug us now, Jack?"

"It's easier for me to hug when I'm sitting down," he replied.

"That hasn't been my experience," Kayla couldn't resist adding, her smile turning into a grin.

"I'd be more than happy to add to your experience," Jack stated, his head-to-toe appraisal making his intentions clear. She was wearing black slacks and a black knit top with a turquoise blazer. She looked damn good. But she'd look even better in nothing at all.

Reminding himself there was a child present, he tore his eyes away from Kayla and did his best to be a good host. To his relief Ashley didn't seem to notice the turnips in the stew. The kid seemed to have taken a hundred-and-eighty-degree change in her attitude toward him.

If he didn't know better, he'd almost think Ashley was taking him under her wing. The strange thing was that he didn't mind her fussing over him.

After dinner Kayla insisted on doing the cleaning up. "Why don't you and Ashley go on into the living room," she suggested as she filled the sink with warm water. Jack's apartment didn't come with a dishwasher.

"Let's play. I'll be the mommy and you can be the baby," Ashley told Jack in the no-nonsense voice of a commander in chief. "You have to make baby noises."

Jack shot a desperate look toward the kitchen and Kayla. "I'm not good at baby noises."

His excuse cut him no slack with Ashley. "You can learn. Babies sound like this…*waaahhh*. That's crying. *Gagagagagagaaaaa*. That's baby talk. Now you do it."

"Don't you know any other games? How about I tell you about the place where firefighters live?"

"Do any princesses live there?"

"Not that I've seen." His gaze traveled to the kitchen and Kayla again. "But I have *met* a princess."

"Sure you have," Ashley instantly agreed. "Me."

She said it so matter-of-factly, Jack had to laugh.

The sound of his laughter warmed Kayla's heart as she stole a quick peek at him over her shoulder while doing the dishes. The open floor plan allowed her to keep an eye on her daughter and Jack. He looked good enough to eat, the gray sweater he wore highlighting his exceptional eyes. And his dark hair had gotten longer in the weeks she'd known him, tempting her even more to run her hands through its rich thickness.

He didn't seem to mind Ashley taking him under her wing and fussing over him. In fact, he seemed bemused by the entire thing and maybe just a tad delighted.

As Jack told Ashley a story about fire and the dangers of playing with matches, Kayla recognized it as one from a book at the day care center. She wondered if Jack had had a hand in it being there. She'd already noticed the safety precautions at the day care center, the state-of-the-art smoke and heat detectors as well as the recently installed sprinkler system.

That was one of the reasons why she'd selected it of all those she'd visited. That and their security about visitors. No unauthorized people were allowed into the area where the children were located. Kayla and all the other parents had an individual code they had to punch into the security system in order to gain entrance from the foyer to the center itself. It was a code Bruce didn't have.

She didn't want to worry about Bruce tonight. Not when she was witnessing magic—the magic of a tough guy like Jack being enchanted by a three-year-old.

"I'm telling you it's an embarrassment," Bruce peevishly complained as he came to pick up Ashley for the weekend. Today's source of criticism was their daughter's vocabulary and her use of improper verb tenses. "She says I's instead of I'm. It's humiliating. I have friends with children Ashley's age who are already using words like hysterical in their conversation."

Bruce made Kayla feel hysterical! Nothing was ever good enough for him. Absolutely nothing was good enough.

"And that bear she carries around is a disgrace," Bruce continued. "The thing looks like a thrift shop reject. It belongs in the garbage. I pay you enough in child support to buy her new toys."

"She has new toys, but she loves Hugs. Don't you dare tamper with that bear," Kayla warned him. "You'd break her heart."

"You're exaggerating, as usual. Ah, there you are Ashley. Come along now, or we'll be late."

"You'll have her back here by four tomorrow afternoon?"

"Sure," Bruce said, but he was already carrying Ashley to his spiffy new luxury car.

A visit from Bruce always left a bad taste in her mouth. Kayla tried keeping busy while Ashley was gone, giving the house a floor-to-ceiling cleaning. By Sunday afternoon she was pooped and ready to hug her daughter.

Four o'clock came and went. Bruce was late. That happened. Maybe traffic was heavy. She waited until almost five before calling him. There was no answer, not on his home phone or his car phone. She dialed his pager number but he didn't return the page.

She tried again and again. Still no reply. Panic set in. What if he'd kidnapped Ashley? What if he'd decided to keep Ashley and not bring her back? Trying to stay calm, Kayla called Diane, needing to talk to a friend. But she got her answering machine instead. It was now after six. What could have happened? What if there had been an accident?

Her skin became clammy at the possibility of her little girl lying hurt in a hospital somewhere. She paced a hole in the carpet until almost seven, each minute taking an eternity. She'd just picked up the phone to call the police when she saw Bruce's car pull up in front of her house.

Yanking open the door, it was all she could do not to race down the steps and grab Ashley in her arms. At least she wasn't hurt.

"Hi, Mommy. Look what Daddy got me."

"In a minute, sweetie. First I have to talk to your daddy. Go on to your room and I'll be there in a minute."

The minute they were alone, Kayla furiously confronted Bruce. "Do you know what time it is? You're three hours late! What happened? Why didn't you call to tell me you'd be late?"

"Chill out," Bruce retorted. "We were out shopping and lost track of time. We took her to this great new toy store in Oak Brook and Tanya got a kick out of helping her pick out whatever she wanted."

"And you didn't think to call me to tell me you'd be late? Do you have any idea how worried I was? I thought something had happened."

"Something did happen," Bruce replied. "Tanya and I talked, and we've decided to start the legal proceedings to get full custody of Ashley."

# Six

―――

"What did you say?" Kayla said unsteadily.

"You heard me," Bruce replied. "I'm going to start the legal proceedings to get full custody of Ashley. Why the stunned look? I thought you'd be pleased, Kay."

Kayla had always hated it when Bruce called her Kay, and he knew it. "Are you crazy?" she retorted. "Why would an announcement like that please me?"

"Because you're totally wrapped up with this new project you went in on with Diane. If we had Ashley, you'd have more time to do that."

"It's a business, not a project."

"Whatever." Bruce's shrug indicated his indifference. "The bottom line is it takes you away from Ashley. She told us how she's at the day care center all the time."

"She's not there *all* the time," Kayla protested.

"Look at it this way, Kay. Just figure that you've been

taking care of Ashley for the past three years, and now it's my turn. Mine and Tanya's.''

"Forget it," Kayla said curtly. "I'm not giving up custody of my daughter."

"You may not have a choice. Which do you think the court would select as a better environment for Ashley? A single working mom who farms her toddler out to strangers, or a loving family with a stay-at-home wife willing to take the time and effort to raise Ashley?"

"I work because I have to," Kayla shot back. "And if you were such a great parent, you'd have taken the time to show more interest in your daughter's upbringing while she was still in diapers. Or were you just waiting until she was toilet-trained and it was more convenient for Tanya to take care of her?"

"Tanya loves Ashley."

"That's very nice. But that doesn't mean that I'll hand over my daughter just because you two can't have kids of your own."

"Like I said, you might not have a choice," Bruce said on his way out before adding, "You know, being in business for yourself seems to have made you even more high-strung than usual."

Unable to say another word without breaking into tears, Kayla slammed the door in his face.

"That was very adult," Bruce yelled through the closed door. "You'll be hearing from my attorney."

The tears were ready to spill over when Kayla heard Ashley's uncertain voice.

"How come you and Daddy was...were fighting?" she asked, correcting herself. "Was it about Hugs?"

"No, baby," Kayla denied, going down on her knees to take her daughter in her arms. "What made you think it had anything to do with Hugs?"

"Tanya told me that Hugs was dis...dis...disgracedful. What does that mean, Mommy?"

"It means Tanya has no taste," Kayla muttered.

"She and Daddy wanted me to throw Hugs away." Ashley hugged the bear as tightly as she was hugging Kayla. "I didn't want to. Do I have to, Mommy?"

"No, sweetie. You can keep Hugs forever and ever. And your daddy and I weren't arguing about Hugs. It's just that your daddy forgot to call and tell me you'd be late, and I got worried. Like you'd get worried if I was late picking you up at day care."

Ashley nodded her understanding.

"Do you like going to day care?" Kayla asked her, smoothing Ashley's baby-fine hair off her forehead. She was getting so big. It didn't seem like that long ago she'd been a baby, smiling her first smile.

"I like to play there, but I miss you."

"I miss you too, sweetie," Kayla whispered unsteadily before hugging her again.

Ashley squirmed out of her embrace to say, "Come see my new toys."

As Ashley tugged her toward her room, Kayla vowed that she'd do whatever it took to keep her daughter.

"What do you mean she's on vacation?" Kayla had placed a call to her attorney first thing the next morning. "I need to speak to her!"

"I'm sorry," the secretary said. "She'll be back in two days."

This news only compounded Kayla's jitters. She'd taken the morning off to spend time with Ashley. Diane had understood and had picked up the slack.

Looking at the pile of expensive new toys Ashley had brought home with her the night before, Kayla wondered if she was being selfish in wanting to keep Ashley with her. Bruce and Tanya could certainly give Ashley more material things than Kayla could. But they couldn't give her more love, and that realization reinforced her determination.

That afternoon Ashley was eager to go to day care to tell all her friends about the goodies she'd gotten. Kayla hugged her about twenty times before leaving. Corky noticed this unusual behavior and quietly asked Kayla if there was something wrong.

"You're still checking the list of people authorized to pick up Ashley from day care, right?" Kayla replied. "And you know that her father isn't on that list. Neither is his new wife."

"Are you worried your ex-husband might try to take her?" Corky asked astutely.

"He wants full custody of her. His new wife can't have kids so they want Ashley."

"Oh, Kayla..." Corky's sympathetic voice was nearly her undoing.

"They can't have her," Kayla fiercely declared.

"I'll keep an extra watch out on her," Corky promised. "Don't you worry."

"You're late," Jack said when Kayla stopped by his apartment later that afternoon. He'd opened the door himself and now he was standing there glaring at her.

She glared right back. "Don't mess with me today," she warned, putting her hand in the middle of his chest to ward him off as an extra precaution.

His irritation evaporated, replaced by something she hadn't seen in his eyes before. Concern.

"What's wrong?" he asked softly.

"Nothing. I've brought the movies you wanted from the

video rental place. And that perfume you've been looking for."

"It's for my mom," he reminded her, in case that was what had set her off.

"I know. You told me that before. What did you do to your couch?" she demanded after taking off her coat, having only now caught sight of the pillows completely askew.

"I was looking for the TV remote control. I can't find it."

"Have you looked underneath the couch?"

"With this cast on my leg?"

"Sorry, I wasn't thinking. Here, let me look."

The next thing he knew, she was on her knees. The black jeans she wore today cupped her fanny like a second skin as she put her head down to gingerly peer under the furniture. The move resulted in her aiming her bottom in the air. The hem of her fuzzy pink sweater lifted, displaying a strip of the creamy skin of her back. But it was the lush curve of her bottom that really captured his attention and stirred his body.

Jack stood there, propped up by his crutches, and simply admired the view. What was it about this woman that stirred such a fire in his body? He'd known her nearly a month and he still hadn't figured it out. He thought about her all the time. Fantasized about her. Worried about her. This was different from anything he'd felt before. *She* was different.

"I don't see the remote control under here," Kayla announced. "No dust bunnies either. I expected to find some the size of Montana. Wait, I see something... Aha, here it is."

In the process of getting up, she smacked into Jack, who was standing in front of the couch.

"Careful," he said, but it was too late. Kayla had been

moving too fast, and the force of her movement sent them both sprawling onto the couch cushions Jack had just returned to their proper place.

He twisted as they fell so that Kayla toppled on top of him. She immediately tried to get up, but he clamped his arm around her waist and said, "Stay still."

Something about the raspy quality of his voice made her ask, "Is it your broken leg? Did you hurt it?"

"Something's hurting all right, but it's not my broken leg," he muttered.

"What's wrong?"

"Nothing that a little of this wouldn't cure," he replied, nuzzling her neck even as he shifted Kayla so she was sandwiched between his body and the back of the couch.

"Hey, that tickles!" Laughing, she wiggled against him, ending up rubbing her body against his even more. There was no mistaking his arousal.

"Tickles, huh?" he growled. It didn't take much effort on his part to gently tug the loose neckline of her angora sweater off one shoulder. "How about this? This tickle, too?" he murmured against her skin before tracing her collarbone with his tongue.

Her gasp of pleasure was his only answer. He could feel the rapid heat of her pulse as he lapped at her creamy skin like a hungry tomcat. She tasted sweet. Like a vanilla milk shake, only warmer, sliding down his spine and making him throb with desire.

Kayla couldn't believe how quickly she'd gone from normalcy to laughter and now to sensual enchantment. She savored the glory of being held by him, the almost forgotten feeling of being touched by a man who truly wanted her. Jack's mouth was warm and wet as he blazed a trail from her collarbone around and up to her earlobe and down again, his tongue creating shimmers of heat with every stroke, leaving her in no doubt as to his desire.

"Yes!" she gasped, as if answering some unspoken question he'd posed.

Gently turning her face so that he could see her eyes, he cupped her chin in his palm, his hand so large that the tips of his fingers reached clear to her temple. "Yes, that tickles? Or just yes?" His husky voice poured over her like honey while he brushed her parted lips with the ball of his thumb.

Breathless with wanting him, she said, "Just...yes."

"Yes is good," he murmured. "This is good, too."

His smoky eyes flared with fire, fascinating her, mesmerizing. He had the most incredible eyes. And she could hardly believe that they were looking at her with such an expression of need while his mouth hovered mere inches away from hers.

He was looking at her mouth. No, more than just *looking*. Touching her with his eyes, devouring her, eating her up like a big bad wolf. But she was no Goldilocks. She wasn't frightened; she was aroused. And she had no doubt she was studying his mouth just as intently, with just as much hunger.

"I can't get you out of my mind, do you know that?" He spoke the words, but she seconded the feeling.

"I remember the taste of your mouth..." Dipping his head slightly, he brushed his lips across hers.

"Do you want me to kiss you?" The words were spoken against her mouth.

She nodded, lifting her head to capture his teasing mouth with her own. Pressed together from hip to thigh, she could feel the heat and the passion emanating from his body.

He kissed her, and Kayla was lost...or was she found? She was lost in the heated magic of the moment as reason and caution were swept away. For that moment nothing mattered but the incredible pleasure of every erotic thrust of his tongue, every nibble of his teeth. But she was also found, discovering the perfect angle of her parted lips against his, inviting the thrill of his tongue caressing the roof of her mouth.

Awash in pleasure, she buried her fingers in the rich thickness of his dark hair, welcoming the increased intimacy of their embrace as he nudged his knee between hers. The ensuing contact was electrifying, engulfing her in a firestorm of desire instigated by the driving movements of his body.

Then he added the additional seduction of his caressing hands, gliding over her angora sweater to steal beneath the hem. The feel of his work-roughened fingertips against her bare skin left her breathless. In contrast to the leashed urgency of his powerful male body, his touch was exquisitely gentle and deliciously seductive, igniting a trail of fire.

The silky material of her bra provided little protection, instead amplifying the heated brush of his thumb against her nipple. She instinctively arched her back and was rewarded by him cupping her breast in the palm of his large hand, claiming her as his. With nimble fingers he managed to undo the tiny pearl buttons on her sweater, pushing it aside to gain him freer access to her curves.

Kayla dazedly opened her eyes to watch him, watch his hands as he touched her. He was devouring her with his eyes again. She saw that before returning her gaze to his fingers. In contrast to the raw hunger in his look, he touched her lightly, skimming the lacy edge of her bra with one fingertip.

His skin was slightly rough as he followed the lacy trail around one breast down to the shadowy valley between and then up the next creamy mound. Kayla hadn't expected that the sight of his large hand on her body would arouse her. Nor had she anticipated how his slow caress would fan the flames throbbing deep within her.

He took his time, seemingly fascinated by every inch of her lingerie until finally he released the front fastener. Moments later his hands had replaced the silky material as he cupped her, brushing his thumbs over her rosy nipples in a rhythmic motion that matched the moist heat pulsing inside her. Excitement built and with it came the need for more...more...

She didn't know if she spoke the words aloud or if he read it in her face, but abruptly he inclined his head. She cried out in pleasure as his mouth replaced his hands, his suckling motion creating a fierce flash of satisfaction as well as a bolt of increased need. Spearing her fingers through his hair, she held him in place as he laved her with his tongue and seduced her with his talent.

As if sensing that she was reaching a new plateau where the pleasure was so intense it was almost pain, he eased back, soothing her as he tenderly stroked her hair off her forehead and kissed his way around her mouth. Then he returned to her breasts, urged there by her eager hands.

His own hands lowered to the fastening of her jeans. His knuckles brushed her abdomen as he struggled to undo the snap. But it proved to be stubborn. Impatient with its resistance he moved on to the juncture of her thighs, where the thickness of the denim seaming crossed over the very heart of her femininity.

Jack caressed her there. First he simply cupped her in the warm palm of his hand, then he began rubbing and rubbing...until that accelerated into a powerfully cadenced caress that had her arching her hips, pushing against his hand to increase the contact.

For Kayla the pleasure took on a harder edge, as the

need for completion grew to almost unbearable propor-
tions. Jack's erotic suckling and rubbing had her spiraling
out of control. The taut anticipation grew and had her
bucking beneath him. A second later he was gone.

Kayla opened her eyes to find him on the floor beside
the couch, swearing a blue streak.

"I'm sorry," she said as she scrambled to help him,
grabbing her sweater and holding it together with one hand
while reaching out to him with the other. "Are you hurt?"

Jack was as hard as a two-inch firehose on full throttle.
He was frustrated and he was aching. And then there was
his leg...

"I'm fine," he growled as he placed one hand on the
coffee table to propel himself from the floor to the couch.
He doubted he'd win any awards for gracefulness but at
least he wasn't sitting on his butt on the floor anymore.
"But I think we should continue this in my bed—more
room," he added with a roguish grin before kissing her.

But before his lips reached hers, Kayla wailed, "I
can't," while scrambling to the far end of the oversized
couch. "I want to, but I can't!"

"Why not?"

Instead of replying, she burst into tears.

"Hey, now, there's no need for that," Jack said in an
alarmed voice. This time his embrace was comforting
rather than arousing as he gently put his arms around her
and awkwardly patted her on the back. "I hate crying.
Don't cry. I'm ordering you not to cry. Ah, hell." He
rubbed her shoulder as if she were Ashley's age. "I wasn't
going to force you or anything like that. You weren't afraid
of that, were you?"

She shook her head, but kept on crying.

"Then what's wrong? Come on, you can talk to me,"

he coaxed her. "And you're welcome to cry on my shoulder all you want. It's broad enough."

"Bra bu bin."

"Bra bu bin?" he repeated in confusion.

"Bruce."

"Your slime bag ex-husband?"

"He's a doctor, not a slime bag."

"He's got the soul of a slime bag."

"He wants to take Ashley away from me."

Jack muttered a few choice curses as he hugged her reassuringly. "No one is going to take your little girl away from you."

"You don't know that for sure. And I can't risk getting involved with you right now. I have to focus my attention on keeping custody of Ashley. If I went to bed with you…Bruce would say I was an unfit mother. And don't ask me how he'd know, he just would. He'd hire a private investigator or something. Bruce and his wife have lots of money. Tons of it. And Tanya doesn't work. He said the court would give Ashley to him because of that, because he was married. There was that case in Michigan where the judge did that, gave custody to the father because the single mother was working or going to school or something. Plus Bruce's in-laws have judges in their hip pockets. It's not fair! Bruce never even wanted a baby. Ashley was only a few months old when he divorced me. He blamed me for getting pregnant. Said he wasn't ready to be a father. I *didn't* trick him by getting pregnant! So Ashley wasn't exactly planned, but she's *not* an accident. That's what he called her, you know. She's a *blessing,* and I'm not going to let him steal her away from me!"

The words were rushing from her fast and furious like water over Niagara Falls.

"Shh now," he soothed her. "Just calm down and take a deep breath or you'll hyperventilate here."

In the ensuing silence Jack tried to come to terms with the roller coaster ride he'd just been on. His body was still throbbing, both from falling on the floor and from sexual frustration. He hadn't planned on things getting so out of control when he'd first touched her. She'd melted like hot wax in his arms. While no novice where women were concerned, he'd never been so wrapped up with one that he'd completely forgotten what planet he was on. She'd blown his mind.

When she'd bent down to look under his couch, he'd wondered what it was about her that so intrigued him. He still didn't know, but he did know that her tears tore at his heart, that her pleasure increased his tenfold, a hundredfold.

He didn't want her leaving when his cast came off. He didn't want her leaving, period. He wanted her in his bed. Since his accident the thought of settling down and raising a family had crept into his mind. Maybe it was no coincidence that those thoughts had started right about the same time Kayla had come into his life.

"So your slime bag ex-husband is trying to steal Ashley from you. What does your attorney say?"

"I haven't talked to her yet. She's on vacation."

"What about your family? What do they say?"

"The only family I have is my mother, who lives in Arizona. She thinks it was my fault that Bruce left me. She loved having a doctor in the family."

Then Jack heard himself saying, "What about a fire-fighter? How would she feel about one of those in the family?"

The moment the words were out of his mouth he realized

that there was no going back now. Even more startling was the fact that he didn't want to.

He wanted to tie Kayla to him with bonds so tight they could never be broken. He wanted to be the one who wiped away her tears and slayed her dragons. And he wanted her in his bed so badly that he thought he might die from the affliction.

Kayla leaned back to gaze at him with startled eyes. "What do you mean?"

"Bruce told you he had a better chance at getting custody because he was married and you're not, right?"

"Right."

"So you could change that. You could marry me."

Her mouth dropped open. Her look of surprise became tinged with a hint of suspicion. "Are you running a fever or something?"

"I've been hot since I met you, but I'm not running a fever and I'm not delirious."

"Marry you?" she repeated with a dazed shake of her head. "If this is your idea of a joke…"

"It's not."

"But why? Why would you want to marry me? I mean, we've never even dated, let alone…"

"Dating is highly overrated," Jack interrupted her to say.

"You've done more of it than I have."

"What about Valentine's Day?"

"What about it?"

"For our first date." If she needed dating, he could give her dating. He could give her passion. He couldn't give her love. But she wasn't looking for love. She didn't need that. She needed a husband. She needed *him*. And he'd prove it to her. "We could go out to dinner."

"Valentine's Day is only two days away. It would be

practically impossible to get a reservation at this late date."
She focused on the minutiae of his last comment rather
than thinking about the larger issue of his proposal.

"A buddy of mine runs a great new restaurant. He owes
me a favor, I'm sure we could get in there. What do you
say?"

"That you're crazy."

"I'm perfectly serious."

"You hate commitments. Why would you even suggest
marriage?"

"We'll talk about it over dinner."

Two days later Kayla had all but convinced herself that
she'd imagined that afternoon on his couch and Jack's out-
of-the-blue marriage proposal. The letter she'd received
from Bruce's attorney had pretty much taken control of her
thoughts.

"Bruce practically bragged that he's got a couple of
judges in his pocket," Kayla told her attorney, Jean Simon.
"I mean, we *are* talking about Chicago here. It wouldn't
be the first time a judge was bought off."

"Don't panic. At least not yet, okay? As you know,
Bruce has filed a request for modification of custody based
on his changed circumstances."

"The only thing that's changed," Kayla retorted, "is
that he's got a rich wife who can't have kids of her own!"

"The fact that he hasn't made good on all the visitation
rights he already has would normally make a judge toss
his request right out of court. But as you say, his in-laws
are powerful people and it wouldn't do to underestimate
them. Usually the court is still inclined to grant a woman
custody if she's been the primary care giver and is not
guilty of behavior that would harm the child."

Guilty of behavior…fooling around with Jack on the

couch didn't count, surely, Kayla frantically thought to her-self. "The court is *inclined?*" she repeated.

"All I'm saying is that when a case goes to court and a judge has to decide, the mother isn't necessarily granted *automatic* custody."

"Especially a judge who is friendly with Tanya's fam-ily."

"I've got a few contacts myself in family court. There *has* to be a judge who won't be influenced, and we'll do whatever legal machinations we have to in order to get him or her."

"Would it help if I was married?"

"Depends who it was to. If you married a jerk, then no, it wouldn't help. If you married a knight in shining armor, who knows? It probably couldn't hurt," Jean said with a teasing wink, obviously thinking that Kayla's question hadn't been all that serious. "Today is Valentine's Day, is that what got you thinking about marriage?"

Valentine's Day! Kayla had almost forgotten. Jack was going to be picking her up at the house in less than two hours from now. The only thing she'd done to prepare for tonight was to ask Diane to baby-sit Ashley.

Since George was stranded out of town on a business trip, Diane had been more than willing to help out, adding her own words of wisdom when she came over to the house. "So the man finally asked you out."

He'd asked her even more than that, he'd asked her to marry him, but Kayla didn't tell her friend that part. She was afraid Diane would think she was hallucinating.

Besides, Kayla felt she'd already dumped enough on Di-ane, confiding in her about Bruce taking Ashley away and what her attorney had said today. She didn't want to take advantage of her friend any more than she had already.

"Yes, he asked me out," Kayla replied before nearly wailing, "and I don't have any idea what to wear."

"How about that burgundy silk dress with the swishy full skirt?"

"I can't find it."

Diane moved Ashley aside and looked into the tiny closet herself. "It's right here."

"I looked through that entire closet... Never mind. Thanks. You're a savior."

"If you don't calm down you're going to poke that mascara brush in your eye," Diane warned her.

"I should have put on the dress first, before putting on my makeup. Shoot, I'm doing everything backward," she muttered, while carefully pulling on the dress. She avoided getting any makeup on the dress, but now her curled hair was all messed up.

Ten minutes later she was looking more pulled together and felt more in control. Then the phone rang. It was Jack.

"Listen, something's come up..." he said.

Her heart dropped like a stone. He was canceling.

"Kayla, are you there?"

"Yes. You're canceling. That's okay."

"No, it wouldn't be okay and no I'm not canceling. No way. I'm just running late, and I'm wondering if you'd be able to meet me at the restaurant instead of my picking you up."

"Oh. Sure. I wasn't thinking, I mean about your picking me up. I know you're not driving yet, I should have offered to pick you up. Or to meet you there. I wasn't thinking."

"I love it when you babble," he murmured with a sexy laugh. "Here, write down the address of the restaurant."

She did, and he made her repeat it twice.

"I'll see you there," he said.

But when she walked in to the Glass Box, she didn't see him.

"Happy Valentine's Day. May I help you?" the hostess, who was completely dressed in red, asked her.

"I'm here to meet someone, but I don't see him."

"His name?"

"Jack Elliott."

"He's here. Follow me please," the hostess requested.

Kayla did, through a maze of tables and rooms until they came to an area in the back, separated from the rest of the restaurant. Normally it might be used for banquets, but tonight it was decorated with dozens of red and white balloons and a huge bouquet of red carnations. "There must be some mistake," Kayla began.

"There's no mistake," Jack said from the table set for two in the far corner. He was wearing a suit and tie. The cut of his clothes emphasized the athletic fitness of the strong body beneath them: the broad shoulders, lean waist, narrow hips. She'd never seen him looking so handsome. He quite simply took her breath away.

"You look great," he murmured, a glint of hunger smoldering in his eyes.

"So do you. Your cast," she belatedly noticed. "Your cast is off!"

"Yeah. I wanted to surprise you."

"Well, you did that, all right." Seeing him on his own two feet for the first time was a heady thing. The man oozed sex appeal. To prevent herself from melting in the doorway, she tried to be practical. It wasn't easy. "Did the doctor give his okay?"

"What do you think I did, held a gun to his head and made him remove the cast?"

"When you want something, you have a tendency to go after it, no holds barred."

"You've got that right," he noted with a wolfish grin. "I've been wearing a damn cast for weeks. It was time to get rid of it. The doctor agreed. Remember, I told you I was a fast healer. But don't take my work for it. Come on over here and check me out for yourself."

His here-I-am-come-get-me look was too tempting to resist. She walked to his side, hoping he didn't notice that her knees were shaking as if she were the one who'd been in a leg cast all this time.

To her surprise he didn't make any more provocative comments, but instead took her hand in his and raised it to his lips. As if on cue, the room was suddenly filled with the sound of a violin.

Kayla didn't know what to say, not that she would have been heard over the sweet, but loud, sound of the musical instrument. They were serenaded throughout their meal, which was comprised of filet mignon so tender it melted in her mouth, tiny boiled potatoes and the sweetest peas she'd ever eaten.

During dinner she tried to make small talk. "Your uncle referred several clients to us yesterday," she told Jack.

"That's good. He must have been impressed by how well you *handled* me."

Jack's grin was so wicked, Kayla became tongue-tied and couldn't say another word.

The violin covered the silence.

Dessert was decadent chocolate mousse. She was tempted to lick the glass bowl, but restrained herself.

The music finally stopped.

"Thanks for your help, Igor," Jack said. "I think I can manage things from here."

"I am sure you can," Igor agreed. To Kayla, he said, "I would do anything for this man. He saved my precious Strad."

"His violin," Jack elaborated for her benefit.

"A Stradivarius." Igor stroked the instrument as if she were the love of his life. "The fire almost got her, but now she is safe in my arms."

After Igor's departure, Jack said, "There's a little champagne left yet." Taking her glass, he filled it halfway and handed it back. "A toast," he suggested. "To keeping you safe in my arms, just like Igor's Strad. You might want to check your glass before you drink that, though," he suggested.

Frowning, Kayla lowered her glass to look in it. Something glittered at the bottom of it. Dipping her finger in the bubbly alcohol, she snagged a ring. A simple yet elegant sapphire solitaire ring.

She stared at Jack in bemused astonishment. "Why?" she whispered. "Why would you do all this—" she waved her hand around the elaborately decorated room "—for me?"

"Because I want you more than I've ever wanted any other woman in my life. Because I felt like it. Because you're worth it. Or you could say it was all of the above," he ended in a teasing voice.

"I'm serious."

"So am I. Marry me."

"This is crazy." But she tried on the ring, anyway. It fit. She took it off again.

"So? Haven't you ever done anything crazy in your life?"

"I married Bruce."

"That wasn't crazy, that was stupid," he retorted. "There's a difference."

"I've got a child to consider."

"I know. And I know I don't have much experience

with kids. But I'm willing to learn. Ashley isn't afraid of me anymore."

"No. She's taken you under her wing."

"Yeah, I kind of noticed that. She's a real special kid."

"Yes, I know."

"So what do you say?"

"I'm still not sure why you're doing this."

"Because I want to. What do you want?"

She wanted him. Her gaze showed it.

"I've been in one bad marriage," she whispered.

"You loved Bruce?"

She nodded.

"That was the problem," Jack maintained. "There's a reason they say love is blind. We don't have that problem."

She blinked at him. "We don't?"

"I may not be able to offer you love, but I can give you two things that are even better. Sex and financial security."

Kayla didn't know whether to laugh or cry. "You sound like some kind of kinky financial advisor."

"As long as I don't *look* like a kinky financial advisor, we're okay."

"Are we?" she asked. "Are we really going to be okay?"

"You bet we are. How could we not with what we've got going for us?"

"Which is?"

"Spontaneous combustion. Do you deny it?"

She shook her head.

"Then marry me. My folks already love Ashley. They'd be in seventh heaven at having her for a granddaughter. We've already covered the sex part, but not the security. My parents invested in some blue-chip stocks when I was born, stocks that have just been sitting there since the car accident, making money. I'm not wealthy, but 'comfortably well off' is the term my accountant uses."

"So I marry you to help me retain custody of Ashley? And what do you get out of it?" Kayla asked him.

"You. And your promise that you won't interfere with my work fighting fires. Sometimes women want to change a guy."

"You could have any woman you want. I fielded the dozens of phone calls, remember?"

"I don't want any other woman. I want you."

"For now. How do you know that would last? It wasn't that long ago you told me you weren't looking for forever."

"I wasn't *looking* for forever, it kind of came and knocked me over the head," Jack ruefully acknowledged. "But it's not like I'm talking about love here, because I'm not. The good thing is that you're practical, you don't expect me to make any sappy declarations of undying devotion."

Not expect, no, although a little rebel part of her did wonder what it would be like to hear such words from him.

"I don't do well with love," he told her bluntly. "And from what you've told me about your marriage, it doesn't sound like love did you any favors, either."

He was right. Love hadn't done her any favors.

"So what do you say?"

She paused for a moment, running through the pros and cons, but in the end following her instincts. "Yes. I say yes."

# Seven

**Y**ou're doing what?'' Diane shrieked when Kayla got home that night.

"Shhh. Not so loud or you'll wake Ashley," Kayla cautioned.

"You go out once with the guy and now you're going to *marry* him? What did you have to drink?" she asked suspiciously.

"Champagne."

"He must have put something in it," Diane muttered.

"He did," Kayla agreed. "This." She held out her hand for Diane to see the sapphire ring on the ring finger of her left hand.

"Well, he's got good taste, I'll give him that. But Kayla, you haven't known him that long. And you're so vulnerable right now, what with Bruce being the swine that he is. Don't you think Jack might be taking advantage of the situation?"

"It's not like that."

"Then what *is* it like?" Diane demanded.

Kayla paused, remembering Jack's admonition not to let on that this was anything other than a whirlwind courtship. The fewer people they told the truth—that there was no love involved—the less chance there would be that something might get back to Bruce to make him suspicious.

Which was all very well and good, but Jack didn't know Diane. Kayla had never, in all the nearly twenty years they'd known each other, been very good at keeping anything from her best friend. Diane ferreted out secrets the way an anteater ferreted out ant hills.

"Okay, what's *really* going on here?" Diane said. "And remember, this is your best friend you're talking to. The one who taught you how to put on mascara, the one who lent you my brand-new prom dress when I got the measles and couldn't go, the one who went with you to divorce court when you got the final decree."

"And I want you as my matron of honor, if you wouldn't mind."

"Jack wants a formal wedding as opposed to running down to city hall on his lunch hour the way Bruce did?"

"I'm sorry you weren't there with us," Kayla said regretfully.

"I think Bruce deliberately waited until I was out of town, knowing I'd try to talk you out of it if I knew what the swine was up to ahead of time."

"I was blindly in love and stupid then," Kayla admitted as she headed for her bedroom and the trinket box she kept there.

"And you're not blindly in love and stupid now?" Diane asked, trailing after her.

"No."

"Then why are you marrying Jack if you're not in love with him?"

Finding what she was looking for, Kayla held up a silver Claddagh ring. "First you have to swear, on our special friendship ring, that you won't tell anyone."

"Jeez, I haven't done this since we were twelve," Diane noted, taking the ring and looking at it fondly. "How do you keep your ring so clean? Mine's a mess."

"Come on. Swear."

"All right, all right. Best friends always are loyal and true, I will never tell on you," she vowed. "Now what the heck is going on?"

"Jack and I are getting married for practical reasons."

"Which are?"

"Bruce has vowed to use the fact that I'm a single, working mother against me."

"And?"

"That means I need a husband. If I married Jack, I wouldn't be a single mom anymore."

"But you'd still be working, wouldn't you?"

"Yes. But maybe not quite as many hours, we're hiring that new person now that business is booming, and that should help take some of the pressure off."

"Business is booming thanks to Jack's uncle, but I still don't see how marrying him is going to change Bruce's mind about anything. You don't think Bruce will be impressed by a Chicago firefighter, do you? If the guy isn't in the thirty-percent tax bracket, Bruce doesn't even acknowledge his presence."

"I'm not doing this for Bruce, I'm doing it for Ashley."

"I thought she was afraid of Jack."

"Only in the beginning. Now she's taken him under her wing and she fusses over him like a little mom. He's real good with her, he just hasn't had much practice in the past.

I think Corky was right, that Jack felt uncomfortable around kids because they reminded him of a time when he was vulnerable, when he was a kid and his parents were killed in a car accident. Since then his philosophy has sort of been that life isn't to be trusted.''

"Do you love him?"

"As Jack rightly pointed out to me a short while ago, love hasn't exactly done me any favors."

"Do you feel anything for him?"

"Of course I do. Attraction, chemistry, fondness, irritation, amazement."

"You don't think all those things could be love?"

"I refuse to let them be love. And so does Jack."

Diane sighed before giving in. "Then it sounds as if the two of you were meant to be together," she noted with a rueful smile. "So when do I get to meet him? If I like him, then I'll agree to be your matron of honor."

The meeting took place a few days later at the engagement party Jack's folks threw for them.

Jack knew he liked Kayla's friend Diane when, within the first few minutes of meeting him, she took him aside and quietly said, "If you hurt Kayla, I'll break *both* your legs." Her tone of voice was both kidding and dead serious. "I've checked around and people say you're a good guy. But you're good-looking and the word is you're popular with women, so I wanted to make sure we understood each other."

"Cheat on Kayla and die, right?" Jack said.

"That's pretty much it," she cheerfully agreed.

"Then I'll live a very long life." Jack smiled. "Listen, your loyalty is great. I suspect Boomer is over there telling Kayla the same thing you're telling me, aside from the fooling around part and in different words maybe, but basically the same thing. We both have buttinskys for best friends.''

''Maybe so, but I just wanted you to know that Kayla has been my best friend since we were both five, and there are times, not many but a few, when she needs some looking after.''

''So what are you two talking about over here?'' Kayla asked as she joined them.

''You,'' Diane replied.

''That's what I was afraid of.''

''Relax. I'll be your matron of honor,'' Diane said before drifting over to the buffet table and her husband, George.

''She liked you,'' Kayla told Jack.

''You don't have to sound so surprised about it,'' he retorted. ''A lot of people like me.''

''Many of them female. I'm surprised Misty and the rest of the gang haven't come after me with an ax for taking you off the market.''

''Off the market? What am I? Raw meat?''

She gave him a saucy head-to-toe once-over before declaring, ''*Prime* meat.''

''Sure,'' Jack grumbled. ''It's easy for you to flirt when we're surrounded by a roomful of people, including my folks.''

''Speaking of which, you were right, Corky didn't think our engagement was strange. She told me that Sean proposed to her within three days of meeting her.''

''They are the exception to the rule.''

''Which rule?''

''That love doesn't work.''

The comment should have reassured Kayla. She wasn't looking for love. She was looking for someone to help her keep her daughter. She was getting the better end of the deal here.

Nibbling her lower lip, she whispered her fears aloud. "Are you sure I'm not taking advantage of you?"

"Not yet," Jack murmured, "but I'm hopeful that maybe later…" He sent her a smoky look.

But later was postponed by Ashley, who came down with a doozy of a case of tummy flu.

By the time Kayla was able to take a break, three days had gone by. The house looked like a disaster area, but Ashley was feeling better. Leave it to Bruce to stop by unannounced. Kayla refused to let him in and instead kept him standing on the tiny front porch. "You're supposed to call before stopping by," Kayla reminded him.

"I was in the area and I saw the minivan here. I thought you worked during the week."

"Ashley had the flu, but she's all better now."

"I should examine her," Bruce declared.

"You're a heart surgeon, not a general practitioner," Kayla reminded him. "You haven't treated any patients with flu since the first year we were married." Kayla had often thought that the reason Bruce wanted to be a surgeon was because his patients were unconscious most of the time he dealt with them, therefore they couldn't argue with him.

"I still think I'd better examine her," Bruce arrogantly said.

"I think you'd better not," Jack said from right behind him.

Startled, Bruce turned to face him. "Who are you?"

"My fiancé," Kayla said. "Jack, this is my ex-husband, Bruce White."

Bruce looked at Jack and then at Kayla. "When did you get engaged?"

"On Valentine's Day," Jack said, taking the steps in a single bound and joining Kayla in the doorway to face Bruce. "A real romantic day, don't you think?"

"I think I'd better check on my daughter. I'm a doctor."

"She's already had a pediatrician see her," Kayla said.

"You can't stop me from seeing my own child," Bruce growled.

Kayla sighed. She was too tired for this. She was practically punchy from lack of sleep. "I'm not doing that. I just wish you'd called first."

Eyeing the spiffy suit Bruce was wearing, Jack decided to try another tactic. "Hey, if you want to see her, that's mighty paternal of you. She's probably done with her projectile vomiting thing, but then you're a doctor and must be used to that kind of stuff. Your suit is probably washable, right?"

"I thought you said she was better," Bruce accused Kayla.

"She is."

"Well, maybe I will wait," Bruce decided with a nervous look at his suit lapels. "I just wanted to make sure you got the letter from my attorney."

"Yes, I got it. And forwarded it on to my attorney."

"Legal fees can get pretty expensive," Bruce warned her.

"That's not a problem," Jack said.

Bruce glared at him. "What do you do for a living?"

"Fight fires."

"Last I heard, that wasn't a real high-paying job."

"I don't think it's ethical for a guy to do something just for the money," Jack countered. "Do you?"

Bruce flushed at Jack's implication. "You don't know anything."

Jack put his arm around Kayla's shoulders and kissed

the top of her head. "I know gold when I find it." Looking at Bruce, he added, "And manure when I see it."

"This isn't over," Bruce told Kayla, his eyes glittering with anger. "Have Ashley ready at two on Saturday for me to pick her up."

"Nice guy," Jack mockingly noted after he'd gone.

"You don't want to come in here," she warned him.

"Why's that? Aha, you messed the place up to make me feel at home. Nice," Jack said approvingly, as he moved a board game, a stuffed elephant and an empty cartoon video box to clear a space for himself on the couch. "And speaking of home, we've got an appointment tomorrow with that Realtor I told you about."

"I have to work tomorrow. I've already been off for three days taking care of Ashley. I can't keep expecting Diane to take care of everything."

"Diane warned me you'd say that. She said to call her and she'd convince you."

Kayla narrowed her eyes at him. "You do recall that I don't like being ordered around, right?"

"Right. That's why I'm going to let Diane order you around instead of doing it myself."

Kayla tried not to give in to the grin he was flashing at her, but it was no use.

"Just sit down and rest a minute," Jack said, tugging her down onto the couch beside him. Since there was so little clear space, she ended up on his lap.

"It doesn't feel like *resting* is what you have on your mind," she noted, aware of his arousal as she was draped across his thighs.

"No?" he countered, the gleam in his eyes downright wicked. "Then what does it feel like?"

"Ummm..." She wiggled her fanny against him. "Feels like someone is up to no good."

"No good?" he retorted with an exaggerated expression of outraged hurt. "I'd say it was pretty damn good…" he murmured, nibbling on her bottom lip while cupping her breast in his large hand.

Kissing her only made him want her more, but he did it, anyway. Just as holding her in his lap this way was part heaven and part hell. Jack had hoped—now that they were engaged—that their bodies could be engaged beneath the sheets. But no such luck. He had to make do with these snatches of passion.

She wanted him, he could taste it in the thrust of her tongue, feel it in the pebble hardness of her nipple against his palm, hear it in those breathless little gasps she made in between his kisses. Her response made it all the more difficult for him to hold back. So he didn't.

In the beginning Kayla had thought that a month seemed like a reasonable length for an engagement. But the time was flying by. Her attorney had gotten the court date on the custody hearing pushed back to May first and was busily preparing Kayla's case. Jack had gone with Kayla the last time she'd seen Jean, and the two had gotten along very well, with Jack contributing some good ideas to the discussion.

As for the wedding…there was so much to do, not the least of which was to find a place to live. Jack's apartment was only a one-bedroom and Kayla's rental house was postage stamp size. It was Jack's idea to look for a new place, a place to buy and call their own.

Kayla was merely humoring him. Not because she didn't want to move, she did, but because she didn't think they had a chance of finding a place their first time out. But Jack remained confident.

He was also looking fit and healthy. She knew he'd had

some physical therapy for his leg during the past few weeks, but he didn't tell her much other than the fact that the physical therapist would give Attila the Hun a run for his money. He'd resumed most of his duties at the firehouse now and would be returning to complete active duty after the wedding.

The wedding. It wasn't sinking in yet, despite the preparations that had been made for it, despite the fact that the big event was a mere two weeks away. But today she had to focus on the matter at hand—house hunting.

"Did you make your list of what you were looking for in a house?" she asked him as they drove to the Realtor's office.

"Yeah." He reached inside his coat and pulled a piece of paper out of his shirt pocket. He'd written it on the margin of the funny pages from the *Chicago Sun-Times*. There were only two things listed, a price range and a basement with lots of room. "What about your list? What did you put on it?"

She reached into her oversize bag to remove her ever-present notepad. She ticked off the requirements with her fingers. "Two bathrooms, one of them large. Southern or western exposure. Walk-in closets, and that's a biggie because my rental house has zip storage space, which has been driving me nuts since I moved there. Also very important is location, it has to be in a good neighborhood for Ashley. Oh, and a fenced yard for her to play in."

When she showed her list to the Realtor, the woman shook her head and said, "You may have to be a little more flexible on some of these, but we'll see what we can find."

They looked at half a dozen places without any luck.

"I told you we weren't going to find a place this fast," Kayla told Jack before they headed back to the Realtor's car for the next stop. "There's no way we're going to find the perfect house, or even the close-enough house, in one day. People can search for months before finding something."

"We're not done yet."

The next house was very nice, but much too expensive. The Realtor was getting testy, and so was Kayla.

As they drove on, Jack noticed a house for sale a few blocks away. "What about that one?" he asked.

It looked nondescript and a little on the small side from the front, but the Realtor stopped and placed a call on her car phone. "The price is within your range and it does have a basement. We can take a look at it now if you'd like. The owners have already moved out. A business transfer. It's only been on the market a week."

"There's a tree in the back," Kayla noted cautiously.

As soon as she walked into the house and saw the open floor plan leading to a living room with a view of a large oak tree in the fenced backyard, Kayla knew she was in trouble.

She didn't realize she'd spoken aloud until Jack said, "Trouble how?"

Instead of answering him, she followed the Realtor down the hallway leading to the three bedrooms and a large bathroom. One of the bedrooms had two walk-in closets. Then they went downstairs, where there was another bathroom along with a fireplace and a finished basement.

"Trouble because this could be it," Kayla told Jack.

"It?"

"The one. I feel sick," she murmured, putting a hand over her stomach.

"Sick? Are you getting Ashley's flu?" he asked in concern.

"No. I think this is the house."

"What?"

"*The* house. The one for us."

"And that makes your stomach hurt?"

"I didn't think it would really happen...that we'd ever really find one that was right."

"Oh ye of little faith," he murmured, putting his finger over her lips and halting her stuttering words. "This feels right?"

Was he talking about the house or the way she felt when he touched her? Either way her answer was the same. She nodded.

"Then that settles it. We'll take it," he told the Realtor.

"What do you think of your new room, sweetie?" Kayla asked Ashley as she showed her the room they'd picked out for her. It was much larger than the room at their rental house.

"Is there choclotts here? Hugs wants to know."

Since it was a special occasion, Kayla had indeed brought a few bite-size chocolates along. Handing one to Ashley, she said, "Aside from chocolate, what does Hugs think of the new house?"

"Hugs likes it okay. Listen! Boomer said a naughty word," Ashley declared. "Uh-oh. Jack said a naughty word, too."

Leaving her daughter in Corky's able care, Kayla went to go see what all the commotion was about and found Jack and his friends carrying a huge pool table in the back door. "Where did that come from?" she asked.

"Storage," Jack replied with a grunt. "We're taking it downstairs."

"Are you sure it's going to fit down the stairwell?"

"Sure." It did, but just barely. And it required some

interesting contortions from the guys carrying the back end.

"It's gigantic!" Kayla said.

"Yeah, I know. Great, huh?" Jack noted like a proud parent.

Kayla just shook her head and headed back upstairs toward Ashley, who along with Corky was unpacking her toys.

"The house is in really good shape," Corky said.

"I want to paint some of the walls once we're moved in, but the ones in here are fine. The Realtor told me it had just been done a few months before the previous owners left. Besides, pink is Ashley's favorite color."

Kayla still had a hard time believing this was all happening. The closing on the house had been at nine this morning, the wedding was at noon tomorrow.

"Where does this box go?" someone shouted from the front door. With practically Jack's entire shift from the firehouse being roped in to helping out, there were plenty of guys to get the work done.

"You go on," Corky told her. "Ashley and I will be fine."

For the next two hours Kayla was busy directing traffic, sending men bearing boxes toward one room or the other with militarylike precision. But toward the end, things got so hectic that no one could have kept track of the comings and goings. The good thing was that with so many volunteers, the work got done quickly.

Things had fallen into place with almost miraculous ease, not only with the move but also with the wedding. A cancellation at the church had freed it for their use. Corky had helped her find the perfect dress, and it was within her budget. Diane and Corky had supervised the rest of the arrangements for everything from flowers to napkins.

Kayla's mother had decided not to fly in from Arizona because her arthritis was acting up. The truth was that she was upset with Kayla for marrying someone in what she'd called "such a blue-collar profession." Given that attitude, Kayla was just as glad her mother hadn't come. She would have ruined things, not deliberately, perhaps, but by her unspoken disapproval of everything Kayla did.

Corky more than made up for any missing maternal support.

Kayla had wanted a very small and simple wedding. But Jack had convinced her that a larger one wasn't that expensive; his buddy from the restaurant could do the catering; the church basement was large enough for a reception. And the guys at the firehouse loved any kind of celebration.

And so it was that the next day at noon Kayla found herself in the midst of a large church wedding. As she nervously prepared to walk down the aisle, she couldn't help wondering how she'd gotten there. The faces in the audience blended together and everything was a blur until her frantic gaze focused on her daughter sashaying down the aisle.

Ashley looked utterly adorable in her flower girl role, dressed in an iris blue dress with a circlet of baby's breath keeping her wayward red curls in place. A similar but more intricate circlet was around Kayla's head, keeping her equally wayward hair and a short, simple veil in place.

As she followed her daughter's progress toward the front of the church, she saw Ashley grinning at her over her shoulder before reaching into the basket she carried to get another handful of rose petals to toss. A number of them ended up on Ernie the Doorman's head, stuck there by his excessive use of hair oil.

The sound of Ashley's gay laughter strengthened Kayla's resolve. She was doing this for Ashley. To keep her daughter from Bruce's greedy clutches.

*And what about you?* a little voice in her head asked. *What about what you want out of this marriage?*

Sex and security. That's what Jack had promised her. Yet they were both about to stand before God and a churchful of people and exchange vows, vows to love and to cherish each other.

Was she doing the right thing?

Kayla didn't realize she'd spoken her thoughts aloud until Diane, her matron of honor, who looked stunning in her own iris blue bridesmaid's dress, teasingly replied, "It's kind of late to worry about that now. Come on, that's our cue," she added as the music changed. "We're on."

"I'm ready," Kayla said.

It was a long walk down the aisle, but Jack was there at the end of it to take her hand in his as they turned to face the minister.

Later, all Kayla remembered was that her voice sounded soft and Jack's sounded confident as they said their I do's. And she remembered him carefully lifting her veil and smiling at her before kissing her, their first kiss as man and wife, a kiss that went on while the minister cleared his throat and said, "Ladies and gentleman, may I present Mr. and Mrs. Jack Elliott."

Kayla found herself laughing, although whether it was from pleasure, excitement or plain hysteria, she couldn't be sure.

The wedding was followed by an equally big reception with more toasts than Kayla could keep track of. Boomer's powerful voice made his toasts especially appreciated by those in the back of the room.

The food was buffet style, with the firehouse chili prepared by Sam and Darnell a particular favorite, among the firefighters at least. And they far outnumbered everyone else. In fact, Kayla could only think of fewer than two dozen guests of her own to invite. But they all seemed to be having a good time. And Ashley was thrilled to have a new pair of grandparents, especially ones like Corky and Sean, whom she already knew and liked.

The sound of a fork hitting a water glass indicated another toast was forthcoming. This time it was given by Jack's Uncle Ralph. "Now I don't want to brag, but if it weren't for me, these two lovebirds would never have met. Because you see, I was the one who first sent Kayla over to Jack to help out my impossible, I mean incredible, nephew. I could tell he made a big impression on her, waving his crutch over his head like a madman. There were sparks right away. And so it should be. So here's to you, Jack and Kayla. May the flames never go out."

"Here, here," the large contingency of firefighters agreed, along with a few catcalls and hoots.

Kayla couldn't believe who stood up next. "This is Ernie the Doorman," he said with his customary deadpan delivery. One rose petal still clung to the back of his head as he went on to give a five-minute soliloquy that nearly put everyone to sleep. When he was done, the entire ensemble applauded...with relief that he was finished.

The next few hours were a blur of Jack feeding her the first piece of cake, of their first dance together and her stepping on his toes, of them being serenaded first by Igor on his violin and then by a group of bagpipers.

Then it was time for her to throw the bouquet. She thought Mindy or Misty caught it, although it almost ended up in Ernie's startled hands after ricocheting off the rotating ceiling fan when Kayla tossed it too high over her shoulder.

The garter fared better, with Boomer making a one-handed grab for it.

The wild dash to Jack's car was accompanied by a rain of birdseed as the guests wished them well. The car itself was decorated from bumper to bumper with crepe paper, tin cans, white paint declaring "Just Married" on each door.

And then they were off, on their own for the first time that day. For the first time as man and wife. Ashley was spending the night with Corky and Sean. Kayla was on her own.

She tried not to be nervous. She and Jack had never actually discussed the specifics of their honeymoon night, other than the fact that they weren't taking a trip out of town or anything, since he had to return to work the next day.

But the subject of sleeping arrangements hadn't come up. She knew he expected this to be a marriage in every sense of the word, except for love.

"You're quiet," Jack noted.

"Yeah," Kayla agreed, but she couldn't find anything to add to that. Her tongue felt glued to the roof of her mouth as they pulled to a stop in front of their new house.

Kayla felt strange wearing her wedding dress as they walked up the front walk. She'd been here yesterday in jeans and a T-shirt. The weather had cooperated with one of those early tastes of spring Chicago got if it was lucky. The temperature had reached the sixties today, and even though the sun had gone down, it was still in the fifties.

As Jack opened the door, Kayla was all set to hurry inside. Fifty might be mild, but not when you weren't wearing a coat.

"Wait a minute," he said. "Aren't you forgetting something?"

"Tell me about it when we're inside," she replied, trying not to shiver as she nudged him aside.

She might as well have tried moving the John Hancock Building.

"I'm supposed to carry you over the threshold."

"You're still recovering from a broken leg. You don't have to carry me in this marriage, Jack, like I'm some kind of burden. That's not what I want. Having you by my side, maybe holding my hand, that's more than enough." She held out her hand to him.

He took it. "Okay, but I reserve the right to carry you over the threshold later. Not that I'm a pro at whisking women off their feet."

"Yeah, right," she scoffed with a grin.

"I've had more experience with the fireman's lift, draping bodies over my shoulder, but I guess that's not the most romantic thing."

"I don't know. The view might be kind of nice from back there," she noted with a saucy look at his backside.

"How many glasses of champagne did you have at the reception?"

"Only two. I preferred the punch that Sam made."

"Jeez, Kayla, that punch is more potent than the kick of a mule. Sam brews it strong enough to make twenty-year veterans of the department weak kneed."

She knew all about being weak kneed. Looking at him made her feel that way. "I only had one glass," she quietly said.

Now that they were in the house, her earlier trepidation returned big-time. Humor had gotten her over the first threshold so to speak, but what was she supposed to do now?

Well, she *knew* what they were supposed to do, it was their honeymoon night. She'd been married before. She knew the routine. Not that her honeymoon night with Bruce had been anything to fantasize about. And not that *anything* involving Jack was routine.

She moved forward and almost smacked into a pile of boxes.

"Relax," Jack said before reaching out and switching on the light. He'd seen the way she'd flinched when he'd put his arm out. "Look, I think the best thing for us to do tonight is to just take things slow."

"Slow?" Images of him making love to her all night, slowly exploring her body from head to toe, filled her head and tightened her throat, making her voice come out in a froglike croak.

"It's been a wild couple of weeks. I don't know about you, but I'm beat."

Immediately Kayla's concern went from her own jitters to his well-being, just as he'd intended. "Is your leg okay?"

"It's fine. But I'd feel better getting out of this rented tux," he muttered, tugging off the bow tie and shrugging out of the jacket. He had the buttons on his shirt undone before she blinked owlishly and muttered something about changing as she headed for the bathroom.

Staring at herself in the mirror, Kayla wondered if she looked as confused as she felt. Leaning closer, she could detect some remnants of panic in her eyes. She'd nervously bitten all her lipstick off, a bad habit of hers.

It wasn't until she tried to remove her dress that she realized how hard it was to reach the tiny buttons marching down the back. She nearly put her back out trying to reach them, twisting this way and that. Each time, she got close enough to feel the button but not close enough to unfasten it.

Not wanting to ruin the dress, she had to admit defeat

ten minutes later. She needed help. And there was only one person around to give it.

Gathering her long skirt in one hand, she returned to the living room, hoping to find him. "Um, Jack?" There was no sign of him. "Jack?" she repeated.

"I'm in the bedroom," he called from down the hallway.

She wasn't about to walk into that temptation. Instead she said, "Could you come here a minute?"

"Sure." He came, all right, wearing a smile and a pair of jeans with the top snap still undone. "What did you want?"

Her eyes were fastened on his bare chest and the intriguing swirls of dark hair trailing from his collarbone all the way down to his navel. Not too hairy, he was just right. Trying not to drool, she snapped her mouth shut and counted to five. "My dress," she said, sounding like a fish out of water. "I can't reach..."

"Sure thing. Turn around." He put his hands on her shoulders to make sure she obeyed his command. "These things sure are small." She looked over her shoulder, just to make sure that he was referring to the buttons and not to any part of her anatomy. Not that there were many small parts of her anatomy. "Stop wiggling," he ordered.

The ivory satin material rustled as he released the delicate pearl buttons from their tethers, freeing her gown so that it fell from her shoulders and slipped even lower with every fastening that was undone. The only thing holding it up was the hand she had plastered against her front.

The brush of his fingers against the small of her back was nearly her undoing.

"There." Now he was the one sounding raspy. "That should do it."

"Thanks." Clutching her dress and her dignity, she

hightailed it to the safety of the bathroom, where she changed into a pair of jeans and a T-shirt, not exactly customary honeymoon night apparel. But then this was not exactly a customary marriage.

"What box did you pack the linens in?" Jack asked from outside the door.

It took them a bit of hunting to find the appropriate box.

"I'll sleep on the pullout tonight," Kayla said, hating the tremble in her voice.

Jack didn't say anything, but he did help her open the couch. He also helped her shake out one of the bottom sheets for it.

She was kneeling on the mattress, having just tucked one corner of the sheet in place, when she straightened and found herself nose to nose with Jack, who was kneeling on the other side, having just tucked that corner of the sheet in. Their hands touched and lingered. The embers that had glowed when he'd undone her dress now blazed into a full-fledged inferno.

A second later they were kissing, intensely, passionately, with no holds barred. Kayla didn't even know she was lying on the mattress until she felt him covering her like a blanket, his powerful body fully aroused.

"Are you sure? I thought you wanted to wait," he murmured.

"I want *you*. Now."

# Eight

Jack wasted no more time. Words were abandoned in favor of actions. He expressed himself most eloquently with a kiss, telling her how much he wanted her, how much he needed her. And if she was in any doubt, the hungry fervor of his tongue echoed the throbbing message of his body.

The time had come. Kayla gloried in the freedom to express her desire, returning his kiss, matching his passion. She'd never felt so wild or gloriously free.

He slid his leg between hers as he deftly removed her T-shirt. She didn't have to worry about his shirt, it was gone already, allowing her more time to enjoy the warmth of his skin, the delicious friction of his chest hair against her breasts, the powerful ripple of muscles. His shoulders were broad, she knew that already. She didn't realize how perfectly her hands cupped the curve of his shoulders, almost as perfectly as his hands were cupping her breasts.

The material of her bra soon became an irritant, because

it prevented her from feeling his bare skin against her. Murmuring entreaties to hurry, Kayla encouraged him to undo the front fastening, showing him the hidden clasp before returning to her own explorations.

She'd never been so fascinated by the human form before. And not just any human form, only Jack's. She found the scar he'd told her about, caused by the ember that had fallen down the back of his collar. Her fingertips soothed the slightly puckered skin, before digging into his back as pleasure streaked through her body at the feel of his open mouth on her breast.

Their first kiss had been like dancing in the heart of a flame. But this…this was like being consumed by wildfire. Not a single flame, but a conflagration.

She arched her back, offering more of herself for his temptation. Jack willingly complied, adding the devilish swirl of his tongue to his already erotic arsenal. At the mercy of her desire, Kayla speared her fingers through his dark hair, relishing the sensual feel of the rough silkiness between her fingers, as the ache between her legs increased to a feverish pitch.

Her hands reached for his zipper the same moment his fingers reached for the placket on her jeans. Words were incoherently mumbled, by him, by her, as his lips returned to her mouth. Their need was so great that even as they hurriedly dispatched their clothing, they couldn't stop kissing.

And then there were no barriers between them, just his aroused heat against her moist pliancy. Whispering dark promises, he rubbed where it gave her the most pleasure, dipped and sampled where it gave her the most delight. The slip-slide of his finger created a friction, a tension, a tightening and then a release that she hadn't expected.

She'd expected him to just take her, not to so caringly see to her pleasure first.

Kayla's look of astonishment and then sultry enjoyment made his own smile all the more wolfish. "This is only the beginning," he assured her, then took her to the heights once again.

Delicate ripples were still traveling through her inner muscles when he kissed her. She reached for him, needing to feel him inside her. She guided him home until the blunt tip of his shaft was poised at her feminine passageway, that hidden place he'd already seduced with his fingers and now filled with his sex.

With one heated thrust he was there, embedded deep within her. She gasped at the rightness of it, even as her body stretched to accept him.

"Are you okay?" His voice was rough, his touch gentle.

She nodded. "It's just…it's been a while."

Jack remained where he was, unmoving as he tried to maintain his self-control. But the feel of her surrounding him was too powerful for him to resist. He shifted against her.

"Don't go," she whispered, putting her hands against his hips and holding on to him.

"I'm not going, I'm coming," he growled, his movements faster now, pumping, sliding, thrusting. He tried to wait for her, but his body was demanding satisfaction. Then he felt it, the first tremors taking hold of her, and then him. Now. Now!

Kayla panted as the ecstasy gripped her with velvet talons. Her entire being pulsated, ebbing and flowing, surging on. Her hair was in her eyes as she watched Jack's face tighten, his smoky eyes dark with raw emotion. He froze above her, shouting her name even as he poured his life source into her. When he collapsed in her arms, her last conscious thought was *Mmmm, yes, I could get addicted to this!*

"Is that a mattress coil poking me or are you just glad to see me?" Kayla saucily inquired before turning onto her back and looking at Jack, who'd been snoozing spoon fashion behind her.

"Both," he growled, kissing her, the lazy swirl of his tongue fanning new fires. "What are we doing out here on this lumpy pullout?"

"Nothing at the moment," she murmured, "but stick around, it could get interesting."

"Mmm, I'll show you interesting." He pulled the sheet off them both and leaped out of bed.

He was stark naked and fully aroused.

"You're right," she murmured appreciatively. "What you've got there is very interesting. And very impressive."

"Then you should be impressed with this." Without further ado, he scooped her in his arms and carried her to the bedroom. He almost walked them both into the door frame as he became distracted by the lush rosiness of her bare breasts.

As it was, he nicked his elbow on his way in the room. Kayla winced sympathetically at the sound of the whack. He then tumbled her onto the bed where they were soon entwined.

"This bed bounces," she noted.

"So do these," he returned, cupping her breasts in both his hands. "I like this one best," he murmured, kissing her right breast. "No, this one is best," he decided a moment later, turning his attention to her left breast. "Mmmm, it's a tie."

Tie...Kayla felt tied in knots as desire returned with a vengeance. She'd never experienced anything like this before; the elemental pleasure, the raw ecstasy, the earthy foreplay.

"Maybe if we changed the view," Jack said. His wicked grin should have warned her of his intentions. The next thing she knew she was perched atop him, her thighs bracketing his hips, her breasts brushing his chest. Putting his hands on her hips, he scooted her up his torso until her breasts were at his mouth level.

He'd noticed the kittenish sounds she made when he caressed her breasts before, and he wanted to explore new ways of exciting her until she purred like a she-tiger. Her husky gasps expressed her joy as he took her into his mouth, suckling her, ravishing her, seducing her with his tongue and teeth.

She writhed against him, the movement of her hips creating a backfire that devoured him as his little she-tiger positioned herself to take him for the ride of his life, coming down on him with silky wet insistence, rocking against him with sultry wildness.

The seducer became the seduced as she took him places he'd never gone before, reaching her climax moments before his.

"We did this backward," she told him much later.

"Not yet, but I'm game if you are," he wickedly whispered in her ear.

She slapped his shoulder in a halfhearted reprimand. "I meant we should have discussed birth control before we..."

"Had sex like two love-starved maniacs," he suggested, with the look of a man trying to be helpful.

"You have such a romantic way with words," she retorted tartly.

"We're married now. What's the problem?"

"I'm on the pill," she said bluntly.

"Don't you want to have more kids?"

"Someday. But I'd like to get used to being your wife and having you as my husband first. Couples should talk about these things *before* the wedding," she muttered, hoping she didn't look as embarrassed as she felt.

"We were kind of busy before the wedding, buying houses and stuff," he teased her. "And for your information, I happen to agree that we should spend time together as man and wife and get used to this marriage thing before expanding our family."

This marriage thing. Is that how he saw things between them?

"Besides," he continued. "I need to practice parenting skills on Ash first."

"Ash?"

"Yeah. It's a nickname. She told me she's never had one before."

Kayla couldn't help herself, she kissed him. Sweetly, gently, appreciatively.

He said, "What was that for?"

"For being you." A man who would be all too easy to love, she silently added.


"Forget putting all your eggs in one place, never pack all your underwear in one suitcase," Kayla declared two days later. "I can't imagine what happened to it. You didn't have anything to do with that suitcase going missing, did you?" she asked Jack.

He was the picture of innocence, not an easy thing for a man with a wicked smile to do. "Who me?"

"Yes, you."

"What makes you think I had anything to do with it? Perhaps the fascination I have with your underwear?" he guessed, his grin becoming downright naughty. "I'm only fascinated when you're in them and then I'm only interested in getting you out of them. But since you've been moaning about your missing underwear for forty-eight hours now, I brought you a surprise."

"I have not been moaning," Kayla denied.

"Don't get me wrong. Sometimes moaning is good. I love those kittenish moans you make when I kiss you here...." He leaned over to swirl his tongue over the curve of her ear. "Are you ready for your surprise?"

"I'm as ready as you are," she huskily assured him, hooking her fingers in the belt loop of his jeans and tugging him closer.

"Here you go then." He handed her a bag from a major department store. Inside were several packages of underwear, the white cotton kind she liked. At the bottom of the bag was another bag, this one from a famous ritzy lingerie store. Inside that was a handful of sheer, silky bikini panties in peach and ivory.

Raising an eyebrow at him, she saucily asked, "And who did you get these for? Me or you?"

"They're too small for me," he replied, tugging her into his arms. "I do admit to being kind of curious to see how you'll look in them, though."

"Only kind of curious?"

"*Real* curious."

"I can tell," Kayla huskily noted, seductively rubbing against him. She could also tell that she was running the risk of falling for her new husband, but there didn't seem to be anything she could do about it. So she enjoyed the moment and decided to let the future work itself out.

"If Jack goes to bed with you, how come me and Hugs can't, too?" Ashley asked Kayla after they'd all been in the house a week.

Kayla was preparing to read Ashley her bedtime story. The little one only wanted to hear "Beauty and the Beast," night after night after night. More recent Disney animated features had come out, and Kayla had them all on video, but Ashley was stuck on "Beauty and the Beast."

She knew the songs by heart, the book by heart, the illustrations by heart. Even so, she wanted to hear the story read to her every night at bedtime. And heaven help the poor soul who might try and skip over a line or two.

But tonight, Ashley had taken it into her head to ask about the new sleeping arrangements, in the middle of her bedtime story.

"Jack and I are married now," Kayla explained. "Married people sleep together."

"Hugs and me isn't married and we sleep together."

"That's because you and Hugs aren't grown up yet."

"Is Jack my new daddy?"

"Do you want him to be?"

"I don' know. Does he want to? Being a daddy is scary for Jack maybe. Would he be mean to Hugs like Daddy?"

"No, sweetie. Jack likes Hugs almost as much as you and I do."

"How come Daddy doesn't like Hugs?"

"I don't know."

"Are you and Daddy still mad?"

"We're not mad. Sometimes grown-ups have disagreements and they need to get things settled."

"And then they don't sleep together no more, right?"

"Uh…"

"Is Daddy going to move here?"

"No. He and Tayna have their own house."

"It's lots bigger there than here. They have a pool. Maybe we can all move there."

"Don't you like your new room?"

"I like it. The closet had monsters," she leaned forward to confide in a whisper. "Jack made them go away, he told me so. He fixed it all. Can I have two daddies?"

"If you want."

"I want Jack to read to me now. Ja-ack!" Ashley yelled out.

"Did I hear an elephant shrieking in here?" Jack inquired a few seconds later.

Ashley giggled. "It was me. Read to me, Jack. Please."

Jack, realizing she'd just granted him a huge honor and that this was a test of sorts, took the book Kayla handed him. It was just a fairy tale. He could handle this. He started reading, his halting delivery as deadpan as Ernie's might have been.

Ashley, however, wanted the rest of the story read with proper drama and flare, as Jack was now finding out when he read the heroine's part.

"You don' sound like a girl, Jack," Ashley was reprimanding him. "Read higher."

Looking like a man being led to a firing squad, Jack fidgeted and cleared his throat several times before starting again.

His falsetto nearly made Kayla laugh aloud. She had to bite her lips to stay quiet. He would not be a happy camper if he thought Kayla was laughing at him.

The truth was she found it so endearing that a man who faced real danger every day without flinching was so panicked by the occasional requests of a little girl. Even so, he was good with Ashley, patient, encouraging and fun.

"I wanna be a bride," Ashley declared out of the blue. "I'm going to get married tomorrow."

To give him credit, Jack didn't so much as blink at the three-year-old's proclamation. "Really? Married, huh? That will come as a surprise to your mom. Kayla, did you know your daughter is getting married tomorrow?"

Anticipating her mother might not approve, Ashley stuck out her bottom lip and lifted her chin in her don't-mess-with-me pose. "You and mommy got married. I wanna get married, too. It's my turn."

"Weddings aren't like birthdays where everyone gets one a year, sweetie," Kayla tried to explain.

"How come? I wanna get married. You get lots of presents and have a party and *big* cake. You can come to my wedding party, Jack, but you have to dress fancy."

Kayla grinned. "Jack looks real handsome when he dresses fancy, doesn't he?"

"I love you, Jack. Now we all live happily ever after, okay?"

"Okay, sweetie." And Kayla thought it really *would* be okay. She'd done the right thing marrying Jack.

Spring was definitely in the air as Kayla reached into her oversize bag for her house keys. It was early April, time to think about putting in the garden she wanted to plant out back. And some pink impatiens would brighten up the front, as well.

Just like the two small throw pillows she'd just found at a craft show would brighten up the couch. They'd look perfect.

Actually the place was really starting to take shape. There was definite evidence that her hard work was paying off. At first she'd thought the job of blending Jack's masculine furniture with her few classy pieces would be impossible, but in the end they'd found a nice balance. His couch had a new denim cover over it and now went well with her birch rocking chair.

And the third bedroom had turned out to be a great home office, allowing Kayla to spend more time at home with Ashley. The business continued to do well, so well that she and Diane were considering hiring another part-time assistant for the errand running while Kayla took over more of the paperwork. The laptop computer and modem she had made working at home a breeze. Explaining to Ashley that Mommy was working and couldn't play all the time was a little harder.

Kayla had resorted to rewards and today had been one of them. She and Ashley had gone shopping this morning and then had lunch at Ashley's favorite burger place.

"Mommy, Hugs wants choclotts."

"Hugs always wants chocolate," Kayla replied as she opened the door and guided her daughter inside.

"Hi, biscus," Ashley greeted the pink hibiscus that Diane had given them as a housewarming present. The southern window beside the front door gave it plenty of light.

That sunlight also picked out the heavy amount of dust floating in the air.

"What the heck…" Kayla entered the living room only to freeze in her tracks.

"Hi, honey, you're home," Jack noted with a cheerful smile, looking completely at ease in a room that could readily have been classified as a federal disaster area. "I wasn't expecting you back quite so soon."

# Nine

Kayla was speechless. The lovely room she'd left this morning was completely torn up. Dust cloths covered the furniture, which had all been moved to the dining room. Plaster covered Jack's dark hair, turning it prematurely white. What he'd done was sure to turn *her* hair prematurely white.

"What did you do?" she gasped.

"Took down the ceiling. Don't judge things by the way they look now. It's going to look great with a cathedral ceiling and skylight. You said you liked southern exposure, and that's what the skylight will have."

"Skylight?" she croaked.

"You bet. I'm going to put it over here." He moved a few feet to his left and pointed at the gaping hole in the ceiling. Hole, phooey, it was a cavity the size of the Grand Canyon. Kayla couldn't believe one man could do so much damage in so little time.

"How could you do this?"

He beamed before trying to look modest. "It wasn't that hard."

"I can't believe this."

"I knew you'd be pleased."

"Pleased? Ashley, why don't you and Hugs go to your room and play."

"Uh-oh," Ashley said, recognizing her mother's tone of voice. "You's in trouble, Jack," the three-year-old warned him before going to her room.

"Now, honey…" Jack began placatingly.

"Don't 'honey' me," Kayla retorted. "You've never called me honey before. Don't start now."

"Okay." He eyed her warily.

"Did it ever enter your mind to ask me before you tore down our living room ceiling? To talk to me, consult with me?"

"I wanted to surprise you."

"You succeeded beyond your wildest dreams," she assured him, tossing her purse and the bag holding the pillows into the relative safety of the hallway.

"I don't suppose you'd care to hear that you look cute when you're mad?" Jack noted.

"You suppose right. What am I here, Jack? A guest in your house?"

"Of course not."

"Then why didn't you talk to me before tearing down the ceiling? Why did you just go ahead and do it as if I played no part in your decision? As if I played no part in your life? As if my opinion doesn't matter, isn't worth a pile of…lentils! We're married now, it would help if we agreed on things beforehand."

"We do agree on lots of things," he murmured, stealthily coming up behind her to nuzzle her nape.

"Don't do that! I'm furious with you!"

"I can tell. I'm sorry. This wasn't some plot to make you feel rotten. I honestly wanted to surprise you by opening up the ceiling and bringing more light in here. You'd said how nice it would be to have a cathedral ceiling."

She wasn't ready to let him off the hook yet, even though his coaxing voice was getting to her. So were his repentant kisses along her jawline. "I mentioned it. Once. In passing. That's not discussing it."

"Okay, so I messed up."

"You've got that right," she muttered, wiping plaster dust from her cheek as she surveyed the mess he'd made of their living room and the damage he'd done to the ceiling.

"My heart was in the right place."

"You don't know when to call it quits," she noted, less forcefully this time.

"Okay, so maybe I got a little too enthusiastic. Chalk it up to the fun I had tearing down the ceiling without having to look for embers. On the job, I've torn down my fair share of ceilings and found my fair share of embers."

"Oh, I'm *very* familiar with embers," she retorted huskily, pivoting in his arms until she faced him. Then she slid her hand down his chest to the placket of his jeans. "And sparks, too."

"Mmm, and flames."

"Whatcha doin'?" Ashley asked from the doorway, making Jack and Kayla spring apart like guilty teenagers caught necking.

"We'll finish this tonight," he muttered.

Later Jack was as good as his promise. When Kayla came to bed after reading Ashley her story and tucking her in, Jack was ready for her. He met her at the doorway, wearing the boxer shorts he slept in. "As I recall, we were interrupted during a very heated discussion about embers and fire. Now where were we?..." He lazily undid the buttons of her blouse, tugging it from her denim skirt. "Ah, yes. Now I remember. I was going to tell you about the basic steps I go through when fighting fire. First I find the fire. Mmm, there seem to be some definite signs of fire here," he murmured as he caressed her breasts, lightly brushed the pads of his thumbs over her nipples. "Now I need to rescue any trapped occupants."

Undoing her bra, he released her breasts from the lacy confines. Soon her skirt joined her blouse and bra on the floor.

"I need to search for more signs of fire." Jack lowered his head to place his mouth directly over one rosy crest. Meanwhile his hands were sliding down to that other area aching for attention, barely covered by one of the silky peach bikini panties he'd given her. "Mmm, more fire."

He continued teasing her with his touch, promising but not delivering. Coming close, but not close enough. Exciting her with his erotic love play.

"I'm going to do these next two steps out of order. I'm going to establish communications—you want to tell me if this feels good?" He seduced her with his clever fingers.

"Yes," she whispered.

"Does this feel better?"

"Yes!"

Tiny shivers of red-hot bliss shot through her, drenching her in pleasure and leaving her weak-kneed.

Jack half-carried her to the bed where he tumbled down beside her, adding his boxer shorts to the pile of abandoned clothing.

"Wait." Leaning forward, she rested her forehead on his bare shoulder while huskily confessing, "I...I forgot to pick up my birth control prescription this morning."

"I'll take care of it." Reaching for the drawer in the bedside table, he removed what he needed. "A firefighter is always prepared."

"I thought that was the Boy Scout motto."

"It's the next step in fighting fire. Taking safety precautions." He took care of it, as she stared at him with eyes still dazed and satisfied from her earlier climax. Once he was sheathed in the latex condom he came to her, nudging her legs apart with his work-roughened hands, gentle hands, seductive hands.

"Protect exposures," he whispered in a sexy growl.

She slid her hands around to his derriere. "Like this you mean?" she asked with a sultry smile.

"Just like that."

"And the last step?" she asked as he was poised to enter her.

"Call for help if needed."

"Help isn't needed," she replied. "I'll show you what's needed." She arched her back and shifted her hips, taking all of him. "Are you…going to…extinguish this…fire?" she asked in breathless gasps of excitement.

"Extinguish it, hell. I plan on fueling it."

And he did, with each slow thrust, with every surge of motion, until they were both utterly consumed.


"What you need here are some real men to finish the job." The proclamation came from Boomer as he, Sam and Darnell examined the mess Jack had made of the living room. Two weeks had passed before he'd decided to call in reinforcements. He'd done a lot of the ground work. Now all that was left was to finish installing the skylight, box in the area, put up the wallboard, then prime and paint it. And the ceiling beams needed staining.

Between them, they should be able to finish things up

today. Jack knew that it was driving Kayla nuts having things torn up this long.

His folks had come over to join in the festivities, and several other of his firefighting buddies dropped by to donate an hour or two of their time. With such a big work crew it was natural that he'd run out of beer.

"I'll go get it," Kayla offered.

"No way. I remember the last time I sent you out to get my beer," he teased her. "You brought back a pale imitation."

"Talk about holding a grudge," she grumbled.

"You stay here and keep staining that wood trim. I'll be back before you know it."

A quick kiss on her cheek was greeted with a great deal of catcalling from the other guys before Jack was gone.

"Did Jack ever tell you what his nickname is down at the firehouse?" Boomer asked her with a teasing grin.

Kayla was tempted to reply that Jack rarely told her anything, not even that he planned on putting a hole in their living room ceiling but especially not about his work. Since that time when they'd sat in the kitchen in his apartment, he hadn't said much more about his work. But she was afraid that if she let Boomer know how closemouthed Jack was with her, that Boomer would be the same way. So instead she said, "Why don't you tell me."

"We considered Jumping Jack Flash, because of his fast moves in a fire, the way he goes jumping and leaping over obstacles. But that was too much of a mouthful. So we call him Ace, because he's so lucky. He was always real proud of the fact that he never broke anything major, like a leg, until now."

Which made Kayla wonder what minor breaks he'd suffered.

"Then we were in this house fire, house fires are always

tough emotionally, you know. Anyway Jack goes roaring into this back bedroom, even though the floor looked like it was going to go any minute. It did. But he managed to save a kid, a little boy, before things fell in. He claims he would have gotten out fine if he hadn't tripped over a hose in his hurry to get out of there. But the truth is that he broke his leg saving that kid, the floor going like that is what threw off his balance. But there was no stopping Jack. You know how he is about saving kids, risk or not. That's just the way Jack is, but then he has his reasons.''

She didn't know how Jack was, at least not about things like this, except that he was closemouthed as a clam. And she had no idea what his reasons for being that way might be, aside from the death of his own parents. Was that why he took such risks?

''He seems to be getting a kick out of fixing up this place,'' Boomer noted. ''I saw he already installed what…three smoke detectors?''

Kayla nodded. ''He did that the first day we moved in. He's a fanatic about it.''

''Because it isn't the heat from a fire that kills most of the victims, it's the smoke. Smoke detectors save lives. There was an incident our first year…'' Boomer's expression became uncharacteristically serious as he sadly shook his head. ''I know Jack has never forgotten it.''

''What happened?''

''It's not my story to tell.'' Boomer looked guilty, as if he'd let slip more than he should have. ''Anyway, Jack put up those smoke detectors because he's trying to protect you. Jack is real good at that.''

''Yes, he is,'' she murmured, silently noting that he wasn't as good at letting someone else protect him. Ashley was just about the only one he'd let fuss over him, and there was only so much a three-year-old could do.

Jack had fallen for "little Ash," as he called her, big-time. He knew as much about the custody case as Kayla did. Whenever she worried about the upcoming May first custody hearing, or "Mayday" as Kayla had dubbed it, Jack teased her out of it. He was really good at teasing. Not so good at opening up or confiding. Not at all.

Kayla couldn't help wondering what had happened that first year Jack had been a firefighter and if it had anything to do with that stricken look he'd gotten on his face when Ashley had called him a monster.

As Boomer went on, telling her about his time with Jack at the firehouse, Kayla realized how much there was about his life that she didn't know—a huge part of his life. It suddenly hit her how little he'd shared with her, aside from his bed. He hadn't shared his thoughts or dreams, unless they related to seducing her.

He didn't talk to her about his friends, his work, how he'd broken his leg or even about the house and his plans to install a skylight. Which left her feeling like an outsider in her own home, a stranger in her own marriage. And it hurt.

Excusing herself, she laid down her paintbrush and went in search of Corky, who was getting lunch ready in the kitchen.

"Did Jack ever tell you how he broke his leg?" she asked Corky.

If the older woman was surprised by Kayla's abrupt question, she showed no sign of it. Instead her eyes were slightly shadowed as if with regret. "All he'd ever say was that he got clumsy."

"He broke it saving a little boy."

Corky's smile was both wistful and proud. "That doesn't surprise me."

"It doesn't surprise me, either. That's not the point. The

point is that he should have told us the truth. He shouldn't shut out the people who love him."

The importance of what Kayla had just admitted hit her with the power of a fist. She loved him! She loved Jack, her husband and a man who'd lost his faith in happy endings, at least when they applied to him. A man who by his own admission "didn't do well with love."

Jack had only wanted sex, and yes, the sex had been great, incredible in fact. But love was something else. Something that took hold of your heart and wouldn't let it go. Something she felt and Jack didn't. He'd married her thinking she understood that he didn't want emotional entanglements.

"That's the way he's always been," Corky remarked sadly, leaving Kayla wondering if the older woman had somehow read her mind.

Kayla's anger, which had been simmering since she'd had to rely on Boomer to tell her about her own husband, boiled over. "Well, he's married now and by God if I can learn how to paint trim and hang wallpaper, Jack can learn how to trust those of us who love him. He trusts his co-workers, so it's not like the man is totally incapable."

Cheerfully waltzing in the back door with a six-pack of Irish ale under one arm, Jack said, "Incapable of what?"

Kayla replied by socking him in the stomach, not hard enough to hurt him by any stretch of the imagination, but with enough force to get his attention.

"What was that for?" he demanded in the aggrieved voice of a man who had been wronged by a woman.

"For not telling us the truth!" Kayla righteously replied.

"About what?"

"How you broke your leg," Corky inserted. "I think I'll leave you two here in the kitchen to settle this. I'll go check up on Ashley. There's no telling what could happen if Sean lets her have a paintbrush.''

"You want to tell me what's going on?" Jack said as soon as they were alone.

"Boomer told me the truth. About how you broke your leg saving a little boy's life. About your nickname. I learned more talking to him for five minutes than I have living with you for nearly a month and knowing you three times that long! Do you have any idea how stupid I felt? I'm your wife and I didn't even know how you really broke your leg. He told me you were rescuing a little boy when the floor gave way beneath you. He said you did that at considerable risk to yourself and broke your leg in the process.''

"Let me get this straight. You're mad at me because I saved a kid's life?''

"Of course not. I'm angry with you for not confiding in me. Why would you want to keep something like that a secret?''

"I didn't keep it a secret. Boomer and the rest of the guys knew.''

"Only because they were there. Why are you so afraid of opening up to me? How do you think it makes me feel when you shut me out? Why won't you talk to me, tell me things, like how you really broke your leg, or what happened your first year as a firefighter that affected you so deeply?''

In an instant his face went blank, although his gray eyes darkened with some emotion she couldn't name—fury or torment or both. Then they became shuttered, locking her out and his thoughts in. "This isn't really about how I broke my leg,'' he growled. "This is about me fighting fires. You've never liked that.''

"What are you talking about?''

"The fact that I'm hooked up with a woman afraid to light plain matches."

Hooked up? His words stung like poisonous arrows.

"Well, let me remind you of our agreement," he continued, his voice vibrating with emotion.

Determined not to let him see how much his earlier words had hurt her, she said, "And which agreement was that?"

"The one where I promised you sex and security and you promised not to interfere with my work," Jack bluntly reminded her.

"I'm not trying to interfere."

"Sure you are. But it won't work. I'm not going to change, I warned you that."

"But things have changed. You're married now. You've got responsibilities, people who love you. You shouldn't be taking the wild risks that you took before. Does being a firefighter mean more to you than being a husband?"

"Yes."

The single word was like a gunshot, tearing through her heart.

"So you just stick to your end of the bargain and I'll stick to mine," he growled, storming out of the kitchen and leaving her alone.

Sex and financial security—that's what he'd promised her. Not love. Never love.

# Ten

With a houseful of company, Kayla couldn't give in to the urge to pull the covers over her head and cry for a week or two. Instead, she stayed in the kitchen a few minutes in an attempt to gather up her shattered composure.

Her movements were automatic as she made herself a cup of tea. Focusing on that prevented her from giving in to the tears that threatened, prickling the backs of her eyes with their insistent demand. If she started crying now, she was afraid she'd never stop.

Pressing her hand against her chest, Kayla felt as if she'd actually been physically injured, but the damage had been done to her heart and soul. Jack had made his feelings very clear, wounding her with the bluntness of his honesty. Being a firefighter came first with him, and she'd better not get in his way.

She tried to whip up some fury, but this time anger

didn't come to her rescue. Eventually, pride did. Lifting her chin, Kayla wiped away the solitary tear that had escaped to trail down her cheek. She wasn't going to make a nuisance of herself. Falling in love with Jack was *her* problem, not his. They'd made an agreement, an agreement that didn't include love, and she should abide by it.

*Sometimes a woman wants to change a guy.* She remembered him saying that, when he'd proposed to her. And he'd just reiterated the fact that he had no intention of changing. He'd flat-out warned her that *love* wasn't in his vocabulary. For once, he hadn't been kidding.

"Are you okay?" Corky asked as she hesitantly entered the kitchen.

Had Corky overheard their argument? Had she heard him admitting that he valued his job over his wife? The older woman's look of concern made Kayla frantically wonder how much she knew. "Did you hear us fighting?"

"No. But I was here when you socked him one, remember? Not that he didn't deserve it. But I didn't hear you fighting. No one did," Corky reassured her. "Not with all that racket of hammering and general mayhem going on in the living room."

"It takes a special kind of woman to cope with this, with having a husband who is a firefighter," Kayla decided.

"That's probably true."

"And I'm not special," Kayla added unsteadily.

"Now that's *not* true. You most certainly are special," Corky declared. "You fight like a tiger for those you love. Are you telling me you're not willing to fight for Jack?"

"All I ended up doing was fighting *with* him. He loves fighting fire."

"Yes, he does. And you love Ashley. Just because you love one thing doesn't mean you can't love another."

"How did you cope with Sean being a firefighter all those years?"

"You just have to have faith."

"I'm not very good at that," Kayla admitted.

"Then you'll need to work on it," Corky said. "But don't give up."

"It's hard not to give up when Jack just told me that being a firefighter was more important to him than being a husband."

"You two were fighting. Never expect a man to admit his true feelings in a fight. If there's one thing I've learned in twenty-five years of marriage, that's it."

"Your marriage is different."

"And why is that?"

"Jack didn't marry me because he loves me."

"Of course he did. He might not say the words, but that doesn't mean he isn't experiencing the emotion. I've seen the way he looks at you."

"I'm not denying he wants me."

"There's more to it than that. Jack has wanted women before," Corky said bluntly. "He never married one of them."

"He was trying to protect me," Kayla huskily admitted.

"From what?"

"From the custody suit Bruce took out to get Ashley. Jack thought that my being married would improve my chances of keeping Ashley."

"Balderdash!"

Of all the reactions Kayla might have anticipated from Corky, this wasn't one of them. "Excuse me?"

"You heard me. Balderdash. Jack might have told you that's why he was marrying you, he might even have convinced himself of that, but believe me he's not as altruistic as that. He married you because he wanted to."

"He doesn't want to love."

"I agree." Corky's eyes were shadowed with regret. "He doesn't want to love. That doesn't mean he *doesn't* love. We both know how stubborn Jack can be, but as I told you once before, he does come around in the end." The regret was replaced with determination. "And in this case, I think maybe you can speed up the process a little."

"How?"

"By fighting fire with fire."

Kayla mulled over Corky's words as she rejoined the others, but by the time they finished working late that night, she was too beat to fight anything or anyone.

Jack had worked like a fiend, clearly determined to finish the project today. It was almost as if he had something to prove.

Kayla had something to prove, too. Several things, in fact. She just alternated between which way to go. On the one hand she didn't want the fact that she'd been foolish enough to fall in love with Jack to blind her to reality. And the reality was that Jack didn't want her love.

On the other hand, she wasn't positive that was reality. What if Corky was right? What if Jack really did love her, even though he was too darn stubborn to admit it yet?

So what should she do? It seemed to her she was at a crossroads here. She could continue to be "the woman who was afraid to light plain matches," as Jack put it. Or she could take her future in her own hands.

Jack was asleep when she got out of the shower. It was nearly midnight, and he'd worked hard getting the skylight installed. And he was right, it did open up the room and make it lighter. Was he right about the rest, too? Had she broken their agreement? Did he long for the days when he wasn't answerable to anyone, when he had a half dozen women with rhyming names calling him on the phone?

Kayla remembered when he'd proposed to her, he'd said he wasn't looking for forever but that it had kind of come and knocked him over the head. That's what love had done to her. Knocked her over the head, but good. Had love done the same to him? That was the question.

Kayla didn't know, yet, what she was going to do about falling in love with Jack. The only sure thing she had to hold on to that night was to focus on the reason for this marriage. Ashley.

"So where's that new husband of yours?" Bruce asked as he came to pick up Ashley for his weekend visit the next day, Saturday.

"He's at work."

"I see he finally got the skylight finished in here." Bruce looked around the room and nodded approvingly. "Not bad."

Kayla couldn't believe her ears or eyes. Bruce was actually smiling at her affably, and he'd said something nice. Maybe miracles did happen, after all!

"You're in a good mood," she cautiously noted.

"I just got some fantastic news."

"You got a promotion at work?" She suspected it had to do with work because it was the only thing Bruce really got excited about. Strange how she'd married two men married to their jobs.

"No, this isn't about work," Bruce replied. "It's about Tanya. She's pregnant."

"What?"

"We finally got lucky. She's about three months along. We never suspected, not after all this time. And me being a doctor.'' Bruce shook his head and smiled. "I don't think she's ever going to let me hear the end of it."

"How does this affect Ashley?"

"Well, she'll have a baby half sister or brother."

"I meant the custody issue."

"Tanya and I have decided to drop the suit."

Kayla almost sank onto the floor. The relief was overwhelming.

"It would be too much for Tanya to take care of Ashley full-time, what with her being pregnant and all," Bruce continued. "So I called my attorney last night and told him to drop the suit."

Just like that? It was over just like that?

Kayla was stunned. The custody fight was over.

Now the tension was between Kayla and Jack.

After Bruce and Ashley had gone, Kayla vacuumed the remaining plaster dust from the living room and brooded over what to do about Jack. Ashley adored him. So did Kayla, which made it hard for her to deal with the very real danger he faced as a firefighter. And him refusing to confide in her only made it worse.

When she'd first met Jack, he'd been on medical leave, and even the month they were engaged, he hadn't returned to full active duty yet.

But now he had. She knew how much he loved his job. She knew he was good at what he did. But she also feared that he took risks he shouldn't. Something was driving him, haunting him, and she didn't know what it was. It might have something to do with his parents' death in that car accident, but she couldn't be sure. She couldn't be sure of anything where Jack was concerned. But she aimed on finding out soon. Real soon.

Jack felt the adrenaline pumping through his system as powerfully as the water pumping through the two-and-a-half-inch hose he held, aimed at the living, dancing wall of fire.

He wasn't fighting this battle alone. His partners were all around him: Sam at his back, Boomer beside him and Darnell behind Boomer.

They were crouched down low where the air was cooler, *cooler* being a relative term. The heat was still intense, permeating every pore of his body even through the fire-resistant turnouts he wore. In an attempt to protect his skin, he'd buttoned his coat collar tightly around his neck and pulled the gauntlets of his gloves up over the cuffs of his coat.

Jack kept his breathing steady, conserving his strength and the air in the SCBA on his back. The hellish red glow of the fire was reflected in their face masks as they beat the fire back. It fought to stay alive, one darting flame leaping up the wall, another dodging over the far doorway.

But Jack was ruthless in his pursuit of the she-devil. He kept the one-inch nozzle open and on target, rotating the foglike spray in a counter-clockwise motion until it killed the fire.

A thumbs-up motion from Boomer congratulated him. It was the only moment of celebration they allowed themselves before moving on to the next step of searching for any pockets of fire or embers that might still be deviously hiding behind the walls or up in the ceiling, just waiting in smoldering anticipation to start things up again.

Thirty minutes later Jack stood outside and inhaled cooling drafts of air. Fresh air. And then he smiled, exhilarated and utterly exhausted at the same time.

He saw a similar look of tired triumph on Boomer's soot-streaked face.

They'd done it. Beaten another fire. This one had been

in an abandoned building, but it had put up a fierce fight before surrendering.

As Jack shared that moment of victory with his comrades at arms, he wondered why Kayla couldn't understand that what he did was important. Sure the building had been abandoned, but they'd rescued two teenagers who'd been holing up in the building. Two more lives saved.

He made a difference here, and that gave his life purpose and meaning. Without that he was lost. His work was who he was, it was so simple. Why couldn't Kayla see that?

Back at the firehouse a few hours later, the guys sat around the break room, waiting for the next alarm to go off. Those who weren't watching the latest action-packed blockbuster movie on cable TV were discussing the ways of the world and of women in particular.

Jack started the dialogue. "What is it with women? How come they always have to try and change a guy?"

Since half the men there were divorced, he was speaking to a sympathetic audience. "I hear you, buddy," said one guy.

"The problem is that women are obsessed with love," another stated. "We're obsessed with fire."

"Except for Sam. He's also obsessed with those filthy cigars of his," Boomer inserted, his voice muffled by the handful of corn chips he was in the process of chewing.

"Hey, if you want to talk filthy, what about those magazines in your locker?" Sam retorted.

"I read 'em for the articles."

"Yeah," Sam said with a Groucho Marxlike wiggle of his bushy eyebrows. "And we know which articles those are. The really well-developed ones, like most of Jack's girlfriends had."

"Jack had the perfect life, and then he went and got married," one of the divorced men said.

"It wasn't all that perfect before," Jack muttered.

"I can't be worrying about this kind of stuff when I'm fighting fires," one man said. "I'm already worrying about taking out doors, hauling hoses, carrying out John Doe who was stupid enough to smoke in bed. I'm thinking about pulling ceilings, ventilating a roof…"

"Yeah, that's what Jack did at his place. Ventilated the roof and pulled out the ceiling. Only he didn't do it because of any fire. He called it home improvements," Sam noted mockingly.

Some more good-natured ribbing took place before Darnell stopped passing around the latest photos of his baby girl to put in his two cents worth.

"I don't know. I think marriage has a lot in common with fighting fire," Darnell quietly maintained. "You have to trust each other not to run when the going gets bad. You have to depend on them being there."

With Darnell's words, an imaginary lightbulb suddenly snapped on in Jack's head as he recalled something—Kayla's comment about Jack being committed to his friends at the firehouse and did he think he'd ever be able to depend on someone outside of that closed circle. And he'd told her then that that kind of emotional commitment to a woman could eat a man alive.

But marriage *hadn't* eaten him alive. In fact, he'd been happier than he'd ever been this past month. He'd come to depend on Kayla being there for him, with him. Did that mean he loved her? For the first time ever, the possibility didn't scare him spitless.

"Jack is still a newlywed," Sam stated. "Look at that stunned, kinda stupid look on his face. He's thinking about his wife."

"If I was married to Kayla, I'd think about her, too,"

Boomer noted with a lecherous grin. "You ever get un-happy, Jack, you just send her my way."

Jack had grabbed a handful of Boomer's shirt and yanked him out of his chair before he knew what happened.

"Hey, buddy, calm down," Boomer protested. "I was just kidding!"

Swearing under his breath, Jack released his best friend with a muttered, "Sorry." Running a hand through his hair, Jack shot a warning look in Boomer's direction as he added, "But don't even think about chasing after Kayla."

"I won't."

"Good," Jack growled, trying to come to terms with the powerful emotions raging inside. The fury he'd felt at the thought of Boomer touching Kayla had been more than mere jealousy. Even though he knew his friend would never betray him, he'd been stunned by the intensity of his feelings. Apparently he wasn't the only one—his co-workers were warily eyeing him as if he'd suddenly grown two heads. "What are you guys staring at?"

"Nothing," they all answered as one.

As Jack left the break room, he heard someone mutter, "What was his problem?" and then Boomer's laughing reply, "If I didn't know better, I'd say there's a man who just discovered he's in love with his wife."

"I came home and found Jack ripping out the ceiling," Kayla told Diane over the phone Saturday night. She'd called to share the good news about Bruce dropping the custody suit, but the conversation had soon centered on Jack.

"So you told me. That's what happens when you leave a man home alone with tools."

"And he didn't tell me how he really broke his leg."

"Kind of a minor complaint, don't you think? Come on, Kayla, what's really going on here?"

The kindness in her best friend's voice brought the threat of tears as she unsteadily confessed, "Jack said he was hooked up with a woman afraid to light plain matches... and...and he said it as if he regretted it."

"Your marriage is in trouble because you won't light matches?" Diane was clearly puzzled.

"He says I'm afraid. And he's right. How did a girl who is afraid of matches end up marrying a firefighter?"

"As I recall, it was supposed to be a marriage of convenience, having nothing to do with love but rather with practical matters."

"That's what was supposed to happen," Kayla muttered. "But I screwed up and fell in love with him."

"Hmm, I can see that loving your husband might be a terrible problem," Diane teased.

"It is if he doesn't love you back."

"What makes you think he doesn't?"

"We had this big fight last night. I flat-out asked him if being a firefighter was more important to him than being a husband, and he said yes."

"People say things they don't mean when they're fighting."

"That's what Corky said, but..."

"How about looking at what the man has actually *done*, by his actions instead of his words? According to what you've told me, he went through a great deal of trouble to stage an incredibly romantic marriage proposal complete with music and flowers. He helped you out when Ashley had the stomach flu and didn't complain or freak out when she threw up on him. He practically eats you with those sexy eyes of his whenever he looks at you. He built a skylight for you and a cathedral ceiling, just because you once mentioned in passing that it might be neat. Gee, Kayla, it sounds to me like he's doing all the things a man in love would do.''

"Why would a man in love say that firefighting was more important than being a husband?''

"Because he was scared of his feelings. When you found out that you loved him, you socked him in the stomach. Not exactly the actions of a totally in-control woman.''

"I barely touched him. And I did that because he hadn't been up-front with me, because there was so much of himself that he was holding back.''

"Socking him doesn't seem to have been the answer,'' Diane noted wryly.

"I know. I plan on taking another course of action. Corky calls it fighting fire with fire.''

"What do you call it?''

"Jack's Waterloo.''

Boomer's words stayed with Jack through the night. "A man who just discovered he loved his wife.'' Was that an accurate description of Jack? A man in love with his wife? It sure as hell was starting to feel that way.

"You have to trust each other not to run,'' Darnell had said earlier. What if Kayla had decided to run? What if she was tired of living with a firefighter who told her his job was more important than she was? He hadn't really meant that, but once the words were out it was hard to take them back.

His shift over, Jack was getting ready to leave the station the next morning when Boomer yelled out, "Hey, buddy, wait up!''

"Look, if it's about last night, I'm not in the mood for

any more kidding around." Jack's emotions felt too new for him to even examine too closely, let alone his buddy.

"This isn't a joke. I wish it was. Jack, the dispatch just told me that there was a fire reported...at your house."

The pallor on Jack's face made Boomer reach out to grab his arm. "Steady there, buddy."

"How bad?"

"I don't know. The call just came in. Your house isn't in our district but the appropriate units are on their way."

Jack dashed to his car and made the twenty-minute drive home in nearly half that time. And all the while his mind was speeding as fast as his car. What if something happened to her? What if he'd discovered he loved her only to lose her?

Jack was too afraid to pray. The last time he'd prayed he'd been a terrified nine-year-old trapped in the twisted ruins of his parents' car. He'd prayed that his parents would live...and they hadn't.

So he didn't pray. He just raced home as fast as he could. Because home was where Kayla was. She was like a bowline, always there, something you could bet your life on. How could he have been so blind? Why hadn't he realized he loved her earlier? Hell, he'd probably loved her the first time he'd seen her, when she'd yelled at him for swinging his crutch at her. Those funny tugs he'd felt on his heart when she'd fussed over him hadn't been irritation as he'd impatiently dismissed. She'd broken down his defenses one by one.

Jack was used to being the one who walked in and rescued people. He wasn't used to someone else doing it to him. But Kayla had. She'd rescued him from a life devoid of a special woman's warmth.

He'd discovered he loved her last night, but only now was he realizing how deeply rooted that love was.

Giving in, Jack finally whispered a broken prayer before turning the corner to his house on two wheels. A fire engine was out front, red lights flashing, when he came to a screeching halt in front of his house.

Jack frantically searched for signs of flames even as he leaped over the pink impatiens Kayla had planted along the walkway.

Recognizing him, one of the firefighters called out. "Hey, Ace, how's it going? What are you doing here? A little out of your jurisdiction, isn't it?"

"I live here." He came to a skidding halt as he saw Kayla standing on the front step. She was wearing a trench coat and her feet were bare, showing off the bright red nail polish on her toenails.

"Well, you can relax," the firefighter said. "It was a false alarm."

"What happened?" Jack demanded of Kayla, even as he took her in his arms and practically hugged the breath out of her. "Where's Ashley?"

He had to bend his head to hear her reply, partially because she was speaking against his collarbone. But he wasn't about to let her go. Not now. Not ever. "Ashley is with Bruce for the weekend."

"Right. What happened?"

"I lit lots of candles, those votive kind. I lit too many, I guess, and I didn't realize I'd set a bunch of the candles right under the smoke alarm until the darn thing went off. I didn't know it was hooked up directly to the fire department. I feel like an idiot."

"You're not an idiot," he murmured huskily, resting his chin on the top of her head as he rocked her in his arms an extra moment before reluctantly turning to the firefighters taking their leave. "Thanks, guys."

"Anytime," the firefighter who'd recognized him replied. "Nice skylight you got in the living room. You do good work. Want to come over to my place and finish my basement?"

"I've got plenty right here to keep me busy," Jack retorted, keeping his arm around Kayla.

Guiding her back inside, Kayla was still muttering about feeling foolish.

"No harm done," Jack said, his voice rusty. "False alarms happen."

"When Corky told me to fight fire with fire, this wasn't what I had in mind," Kayla noted.

"What did you have in mind?"

"This." She unbelted her nondescript trenchcoat to reveal the fire engine red teddy she was wearing, an incredibly sexy piece of nothing that revealed more than it covered. The plunging neckline went almost to her navel, while the high-cut lace showed off her thighs.

Jack just stared at her, slack-jawed, before blurting out, "I love you." The statement came tumbling from his lips in one continuous word.

Frowning at him, she wrapped the coat around herself again. "Are you making fun of me?" she demanded with a primness that made him long to kiss her.

"No. No way! Believe me, I didn't want to love you. I fought it as hard and as long as I could," he muttered. "And I was doing a pretty good job of it, too, until Boomer told me that a fire had been reported here. Then…then I knew. If anything had happened to you…"

He tugged her back into his arms again.

Kayla drew his head down so she could look into his smoky eyes, searching for the truth and finding it there. "You mean you really *do* love me?" she whispered.

"Yeah." He ran his work-roughened fingertips across her forehead, down her cheek, over the stubborn tilt of her jaw and back up her other cheek—as if drawing an invisible frame around her face. "What about you?"

Her smile was both radiant and shaky. "I knew I loved you when I socked you in the stomach."

"That was your way of showing me that you loved me?"

"No." She turned her head to kiss his palm. "No. I shouldn't have done that."

"And I shouldn't have said some of the things that I did. Fighting fire is my life, Kayla. But so are you. One isn't more important than the other. I was angry when I said that. I was fighting my feelings for you."

"Why did you fight it?" she asked in a small voice. "Did you think it would be so bad to love me?"

"Loving anyone scared the bejesus out of me."

"Why? Is it because of your parents' deaths?"

Sighing, he realized that she wasn't going to be happy until she'd heard it all. "Yeah. I loved them and they left. It's not rational, maybe, but that's how I felt. You love someone, they end up getting taken away from you. I vowed then and there that I was going to be tough. I wasn't ever going to be hurt like that again, never allow myself to get that dependent on someone else. It was a vow I kept, even when Corky and Sean adopted me."

"Because admitting you loved them might mean having them leave you?"

"Yeah."

"What about now? Do you believe in love now? Do you believe that I love you, despite the fact that you're the most stubbornly mule-headed man I've ever met? I love you, anyway. You are worthy of being loved. You don't have to keep proving yourself. You're already a hero."

"I'm not a hero. I'm just a man doing his job. It's what I do. It's what I am."

"No one takes more risks than you do. Why is that?"

"Maybe I'm trying to make up for past mistakes."

"What past mistakes?"

"The car accident. With my parents. It was my fault." The harsh words were torn out of him.

"How could that be? You were just a kid, sleeping in the back seat."

"I wasn't asleep. I was acting up. I was tired of being cooped up in the car. The drive from Springfield had seemed to take forever. My father looked over his shoulder at me. That's why he didn't see the car coming at us. Later I was told it was a miracle I was spared. I figured I must have been saved for a reason and that reason was to make a difference, to help others. I wanted to be a firefighter to make up for what I'd done wrong."

"You didn't do anything wrong."

"There's more." A muscle in his jaw throbbed, a visible sign of his emotions, emotions he was trying to keep in check. "My first year in the department, I made another mistake. There was this kid, no bigger than Ashley, hiding under his bed. I was wearing my breathing apparatus, the smoke was thick enough to cut in there. I saw the kid, reached for him. But he was frightened of me, he thought I was some kind of monster coming to get him. I heard him scream 'Monster' and then saw him crawl out from the other side of the bed, right into the flames. There was no saving him."

"Oh, Jack. I'm so sorry." She slid her arms around his back.

For a moment he tensed against her. The years of automatically rejecting comfort and love were tough to break, and she was fearful that he might push her away. Then, with a sudden groan, he pulled her close, dropping his forehead to her shoulder.

Kayla blinked away the tears as she tenderly stroked his dark hair with her fingers. At first she expressed her loving compassion simply with her touch.

After a few moments had passed, she spoke. "You just said it yourself, Jack. There was no saving that little boy. Just as there was no saving your parents in that car accident. Things happen, tragic things happen, but they aren't your fault. You didn't do anything wrong. You didn't set the fire that killed that child."

His voice was ragged as he said, "No, but I didn't save him, either."

"So you've been trying to make up for it ever since by risking your own life to save a child's. Oh, Jack, don't you see? You have to let go of the past. You've got to be willing to move ahead, to know that there are people who love you. To trust in that love."

"What if I don't deserve it?"

"Don't say that!" She tugged on his hair in a gentle but firm reprimand.

Lifting his head, he stared into her eyes. They were as blue as the heart of a flame, he belatedly realized. He'd been searching since the day he'd first met her for a way to describe her eyes. Now he'd found it.

Her eyes flashed fire at him as her look turned into a glare. "You *do* deserve to be loved, dammit! You just have to be willing to reach out your hand and grab it, take that risk. That shouldn't be so difficult for a man used to living on the edge."

"Keep talking." His voice was thick with emotion as he tucked a loose strand of her honey brown hair behind her ear.

"Remember what you told me about fire, that you had to learn about it, respect it and make it your friend, to do your job? Well, how about doing that with love? Learn about it, respect it and make it your friend instead of your enemy.''

"And how do I do that?''

"I can help you.''

"I'm sure you can. But I already learned a thing or two on my own.''

"Like what?''

"Like the fact that my life would be dark and empty without you. Like the fact that even though you're bossy and you hog all the mushrooms on a pizza, I love you.''

Her smile was glorious as she said, "Tell me again.''

"You're bossy and you hog—''

"I meant the last part.''

"You're going to make me say it again?''

"You bet I am. A hundred times a day, until it comes as naturally to you as ripping out ceilings.''

"A hundred times a day?''

His exaggerated look of horror cracked her up. "Okay, ten times a day,'' she said.

"Twice, maybe. A week.''

"Four times a day and that's my final offer.''

"I accept.''

The words were spoken against her mouth as he kissed her. The wealth of emotion expressed brought tears to her eyes. There had always been passion before, always been hunger and need. There had even been tenderness and gentleness. But now there was love. Love that no longer had to be kept hidden, no longer had to be fought.

His arms cradled her, wrapping her in their protective warmth, surrounding, encircling her. She loved him so much, and the freedom to tell him, to show him, was powerful and heady.

"Remember when you told me you were an expert with knots?'' Kayla huskily asked.

"Mmm," he mumbled as he grappled with the knot on the belt of her trench coat while she backed down the hallway toward their bedroom, carefully avoiding the trail of unlit scented candles.

"Maybe you could teach me some of those fancy knots. Who knows, I might get creative and want to experiment with tying you to the headboard of the bed."

By now she'd led him into their bedroom. Bright-colored scarves were draped over the lamps and the headboard, lending the room an exotic look. She also had some kind of bright material draped over the windows, while jewel-colored pillows were strewn across the floor, their brilliance enhanced by the burgundy silk bottom sheet. None of this had been here when he'd left for work.

Jack looked around in disbelief and awe. "What is this, a harem?"

"That was the general idea, yes. That's why there was a trail of tons of candles in the hallway, which I'll have you know I lit with plain matches, not safety matches. Well, I lit most of them that way."

"You had all this planned?"

"Except for the fire department arriving," she ruefully replied. "There's only one firefighter I'm interested in. And I'm interested in seeing more of him," she added, unbuttoning first his shirt and then reaching for the zipper on his jeans. "A *lot* more of him."

When their clothing was gone, Jack was still murmuring, "I can't believe this."

"Believe it. Okay, now stretch out on the bed. No wait, I still don't know how to tie those knots yet. You have to show me…"

Tumbling her down onto the bed bedside him, Jack flashed her a grin worthy of any roguish knight. "I've got plenty to show you, princess. Right here…"

He guided her fingers to his fully aroused body where she was distracted from her original plan by the feel of him, taut and velvety strong, in her hand.

The need to be close, to be as one, was overwhelming. Kissing her once again, Jack growled his pleasure as she caressed him. The brush of his chest hair against her nipples was a delicious torment, making her want more.

Jack gave it to her, his hands doing more giving than taking, his lips more adoring than provoking. He caressed every secret, intimate, sensitive part of her body. The soft assault drenched her in joy.

By the time he slid into her warm, slick recesses to bury himself in her, Kayla knew what it was to be cherished, to be truly loved. As he rocked against her, the blissful excitement grew, lifting her upward, expanding her universe before telescoping it inward into the most exquisite ecstasy possible. Rippling, surging, ebbing and flowing as her entire being reached, reached and then attained total satisfaction.

It took them both some time to come back to earth, and even then they basked awhile in a hazy afterglow that Kayla adored as she snuggled against her husband.

Tenderly combing his fingers through her hair, Jack murmured, "All my life I've been looking for something. I never knew what it was. Maybe you were what I was looking for."

"There's no *maybe* about it."

"No maybes," Jack agreed, tipping up her chin to kiss her lips. "Just love."

\*    \*    \*    \*    \*

**SILHOUETTE**

*Desire*

# COMING NEXT MONTH

### THE PATIENT NURSE  Diana Palmer

*Man of the Month*

Noreen Kensington knew that surgeon Ramon Cortero blamed her for the death of his wife—so he was the one man she didn't want rescuing her now that she was ill. But would his seductive bedside manner be enough to change her mind?

### THE ENGAGEMENT PARTY  Barbara Boswell

*Always a Bridesmaid!*

After three proposals but not one wedding, Hannah Farley had sworn off men forever. But Matthew Granger intrigued her—what was he hiding? Hannah was determined to tempt his secrets from him—and lure him up the aisle!

### WIFE BY CONTRACT  Raye Morgan

When mail-order bride Chynna Sinclair arrived in town with her children, she thought Joe Camden was perfect husband *and* daddy material. Trouble was, it was Joe's *brother* she'd already promised to marry...!

### THE MIDNIGHT RIDER TAKES A BRIDE
### Christine Rimmer

Adora Beaudine was expected to settle down and be respectable—but instead she was about to say 'I do' to outlaw Jed Ryder. She insisted it was for the sake of his little sister—and *nothing* to do with the *un*respectable way he made her feel...

### ANYBODY'S DAD  Amy Fetzer

Although Chase Madison was the father of her baby—courtesy of his sperm-bank deposit—Tessa Lightfoot didn't want to share the baby with anyone, least of all a complete stranger. But Chase was determined—together they'd make a family!

### THE HONEYMOON HOUSE  Patty Salier

When Danielle Ford was forced to live with her colleague, Paul Richards, she anticipated that he would get under her skin—but not under her sheets! She didn't think he was her Mr Right—so Paul decided to show her just how wrong she was...

**On sale from 24th April 1998**

# COMING NEXT MONTH FROM

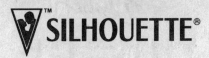 SILHOUETTE®

## Sensation
*A thrilling mix of passion, adventure and drama*

**A MAN TO TRUST** Justine Davis
**CONVINCING JAMEY** Marilyn Pappano
**MAGGIE'S MAN** Alicia Scott
**HER IDEAL MAN** Ruth Wind

## Intrigue
*Danger, deception and desire*

**HIS SECRET SIDE** Pamela Burford
**THIS LITTLE BABY** Joyce Sullivan
**KRYSTAL'S BODYGUARD** Molly Rice
**THE REDEMPTION OF DEKE SUMMERS** Gayle Wilson

## Special Edition
*Satisfying romances packed with emotion*

**THE SECRET WIFE** Susan Mallery
**PALE RIDER** Myrna Temte
**WANTED: HUSBAND, WILL TRAIN** Marie Ferrarella
**MRS RIGHT** Carole Halston
**BEAUTY AND THE GROOM** Lorraine Carroll
**LONE STAR LOVER** Gail Link

On sale from 24th April 1998

# 4 FREE

## books and a surprise gift!

We would like to take this opportunity to thank you for reading this Silhouette® book by offering you the chance to take FOUR more specially selected titles from the Desire™ series absolutely FREE! We're also making this offer to introduce you to the benefits of the Reader Service™—

- ★ FREE home delivery
- ★ FREE gifts and competitions
- ★ FREE monthly newsletter
- ★ Books available before they're in the shops
- ★ Exclusive Reader Service discounts

Accepting these FREE books and gift places you under no obligation to buy; you may cancel at any time, even after receiving your free shipment. Simply complete your details below and return the entire page to the address below. *You don't even need a stamp!*

**YES!** Please send me 4 free Desire books and a surprise gift. I understand that unless you hear from me, I will receive 6 superb new titles every month for just £2.50 each, postage and packing free. I am under no obligation to purchase any books and may cancel my subscription at any time. The free books and gift will be mine to keep in any case.

D8XE

Ms/Mrs/Miss/Mr..................................Initials ......................................
BLOCK CAPITALS PLEASE

Surname ..................................................................................................

Address ..................................................................................................

.................................................................................................................

........................................................Postcode..................................

**Send this whole page to:**
THE READER SERVICE, FREEPOST, CROYDON, CR9 3WZ
(Eire readers please send coupon to: P.O. BOX 4546, DUBLIN 24.)

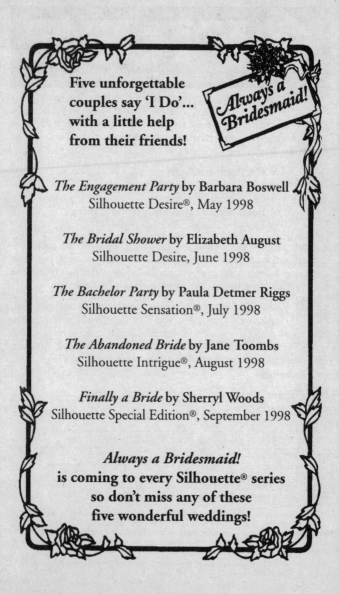

Five unforgettable couples say 'I Do'... with a little help from their friends!

*Always a Bridesmaid!*

*The Engagement Party* by Barbara Boswell
Silhouette Desire®, May 1998

*The Bridal Shower* by Elizabeth August
Silhouette Desire, June 1998

*The Bachelor Party* by Paula Detmer Riggs
Silhouette Sensation®, July 1998

*The Abandoned Bride* by Jane Toombs
Silhouette Intrigue®, August 1998

*Finally a Bride* by Sherryl Woods
Silhouette Special Edition®, September 1998

*Always a Bridesmaid!*
is coming to every Silhouette® series
so don't miss any of these
five wonderful weddings!